Dedicated to Dennie,

who makes my heart sing

Taken by Storm: Galveston 1900

by Ann M. Pearson

To: Sue
Thanks for your
love of reading!
Enjoy!
Ann M. Pearson
April 18, 2015

Editorial Resources, Inc.

All rights reserved.

2014

ISBN 0-9745923-1-5

Prologue

He was with God in the beginning. John 1:2

So many lives changed that long, wild night in the early autumn of 1900 when they experienced the spectacle of the earth, the sea, and a raging wind battling each other for supremacy. Beyond the ungodly sounds as houses crashed into neighboring houses, splintering on impact; beyond the deadly speed of foaming water trapped and rising above gardens and stairs and into homes, churches, and shops; beyond the bewildering images of whole trees floating by the supposedly safe havens of attic windows, swirling currents vying to control assorted debris; even beyond the recognition that no one who survived this melee would ever be the same; beyond all this, they were awestruck with the beauty. The sheer power of the forces at work that night in Galveston bowed the observers into a stupor at God's might. One day, a typical, muggy trudge toward the end of a long, hot summer; the next, a nightmare.

Shortly after The Storm passed into history, observers flocked to Galveston, some motivated by pity, others morbidly curious. They all came with questions. Many were too polite to ask and left quietly, keeping their thoughts and doubts to themselves, as one does at a funeral of a mere acquaintance. Others who presumed an intimacy that may or may not have existed voiced their inquiries. What would a city that had survived the worst natural disaster in the nation's history look like? Would they even recognize their once-familiar haunts? How would the beach that had been strewn with the bodies of 8,000 souls appear now? Could the Jewel of the Gulf Coast ever shine again or would she remain the buried treasure of legend, a skeletal ghost of her former beauty?

But if asked about her before the hurricane, those who knew the island as home and sanctuary, those who loved Galveston as one loves an injured child could only sigh and sometimes weep. The contrast was so stark; the image cut through their minds with razor sharp edges. There's a sympathy in the air now—even after the monumental reconstruction of the island. It's a beautiful place now certainly, but it could never be the same.

Looking back, it would be too easy for the survivors to forget the intensity, the unrelenting black of the unknown as they endured the eerie moments and hours of the darkest night, then staggered through the first days of chaos into the weeks of interminable numbness The Storm left behind. That's what many were doing—or trying to do. They left at the first opportunity; walked away from the smoke and the smells. The sounds of stunned angst. The heaps of rubble. The ruined furniture. The debris piles topped with a child's toy. The rotting corpses. Those who left took nothing and didn't look back.

Tom McDermott couldn't forget though—didn't want to forget. And he wouldn't leave. It was in that grey gloom, in some imperceptible-at-the-time moment when he grasped why he existed and why he had to survive the unsurvivable.

1.   Before the Beginning

...from the beginning, before the world began. Proverbs
8:22-24

It is a truth universally acknowledged, that a single man, regardless of the fortune in his possession, or lack thereof, who is in pursuit of priestly robes must not also be in want of a wife. It just is. Tom McDermott wasn't in want of a wife or at least he didn't know he was.

The conversation that started Tom's journey to that alternate reality was a familiar one in his memory because it was so different from any other discussion he had ever experienced. It was 1896, and he was in his boyhood home. The McDermotts lived in a part of Boston that once had been elegant, but now lost all pretense of sophistication hemmed in as it was by nondescript manufacturing concerns and tawdry storefronts. One grey stoned façade now collided into another with no attempt at distinction—no desire to attract the once-oft appreciative glance from passersby. The acrid smell of the molasses factory several blocks away cast a pungent aura over all their memories.

"Well, Tom. I'm proud of you. You've graduated near the top of your class, Lad. That's no easy task," Uncle Tim clapped Tom's back as they left the crowded dining room after the noisy family dinner that marked the celebration for Tom's graduation from the small teacher's college he had attended just after high school. They all knew this was merely a stepping stone in his mother Katherine's ambitious machinations.

Katherine had controlled Tom's entire upbringing to focus his sights on embracing the sacrament of the priesthood. She pinned all her hopes on Tom as the one child she dutifully bore of so many who would fulfill some notion she had of payback, of balancing her scales to account for her bountiful blessings or atone for her unspoken sins. He would be her offering to God.

Tom McDermott was not alone in being sorted into a life not of his choosing; his mother routinely ticked off her children's set roles to anyone willing to hear. Going back several generations in Ireland and more recently in Boston, the Fitzgeralds held the curious distinction of filling the professional ranks with brothers. Katherine allotted her boys to the time-tested slots: Thomas would be the priest; Daniel, a year and two months older, would go to sea, as all Fitzgerald first born sons had done for ages. Then Sean, exactly 18 months younger than Tom, would go in for law, and wee Patrick, still resembling a slender girl with his long rusty curls and short pants, would stay near his aging parents conquering the mysteries of medicine to care for and comfort them in their dotage. That Tom and his brothers were not Fitzgerald men, rather McDermotts on their father's side, never entered into the conversation. Katherine rarely bothered with insignificant details. The well-known fact that this inherited game of destiny roulette was fraught with Fitzgerald men who despised their chosen path so much that far too many escaped it in drink or through immigration was not discussed either.

Tom's five sisters would, of course, marry and learn the anxiety of a mother's heart, but Katherine Fitzgerald McDermott scarcely cast a thought over her girls. Their good maternal stock and a childhood of forced domestic servitude would stand them in good stead. No, it was the boys for whom Katherine schemed and plotted.

Her marriage to Tom's father, Martin Sullivan McDermott, was not entirely unhappy and certainly had been intentional on her part. She cared little that Sully was no taller than she—shorter even when she wore her patens; nor did she worry that the sun and wind had hardened his face exacerbating the pocs it bore from a now-forgotten battle against early death. Kitty had deliberately chosen a McDermott boy—and Sully was the most docile of all his many brothers—because she knew she could control him and live the life she desired as an active contributor to the ancient Fitzgerald clan. So when Katherine retained her maiden name upon her marriage, neatly penning it in the parish register without hesitation and later included it on all birth records preceding her husband's name as the official name her children bore, the young Sully did not question his strong-willed wife. In fact, he never questioned her.

As did his father, Tom accepted his mother's decisions with no argument. Tom was an authority trainee and had dutifully mastered submission and acceptance as a matter of course. He willingly resigned himself to a life he thought he understood from having watched so many religious examples as he grew up, including Uncle Tim.

One night Uncle Tim spoke to Tom and his parents not in his familiar avuncular role but rather as their personal spiritual advisor as well as the exalted Archbishop of Boston. For reasons Tom could not then understand, Uncle Tim suggested Tom delay his entrance into the world he knew as a priest.

What was so radical about this announcement was that everyone knew Tom would become a priest. No one questioned it. Weak still from the labor of bringing Tom into the world, his mother Katherine recounted often as he grew up, she had risen to inscribe

Tom's name in the huge, unread, but stoically ceremonial family Bible. That very day, she recorded his name both under births and ordinations. From the first hours of Tom's life, his mother had pronounced his future. No one need ask Tom to decide anything concerning his future. Katherine had long before done that for him. For a mere mortal to suggest otherwise was as blasphemous as laughing aloud during Mass.

Actually, *suggest* isn't the correct term for what happened, but Tom did recall that Uncle Tim fashioned it in the form of a question, almost as an afterthought. Tom's parents would never have accepted this alternative for their son without Uncle Tim's insistence; he knew Tom's mother well indeed. And Tom's father merely followed her lead in all matters relating to the children. They were her province entirely.

Without it being spoken, Tom knew Uncle Tim had used up the entire store of resigned acceptance his mother held for his rank, lifelong friendship, and spiritual position in forcing this change through on that night. And even in her resignation, she couldn't quite give up her dream gracefully. The images of that struggle were etched on Tom's memory as if it were yesterday.

Uncle Tim was Boston's Archbishop Timothy Ryan O'Rourke, not actually a true uncle, but a close friend who had grown up with Tom's parents before marrying them and baptizing all of their children as a priest and then bishop. He was often at their large dinner table; and he played a significant role in the lives of Tom's brothers and sisters, finding suitable schools and jobs, and later acceptable mates from his network of contacts. He seemed driven to contribute to their lives and was always in their midst. The entire family felt special with this attention from such a well-loved, important man, and Tom remembered feeling happy Uncle Tim could have a part in the family to make up for the fact that he didn't have one of his own. Tom's mother encouraged the connection all the children felt toward Uncle Tim.

Tom's mother nodded her command when Uncle Tim asked the smaller children to leave the adults alone as the older girls automatically finished clearing the table. The brownstone was large enough for the whole family, but just. Katherine picked up a nondescript ball of yarn and began the knitting she seemed never to finish; her hands rarely idle. Tom's parents sat beside each other on a small divan long past its prime, close but not touching. Tom had a random thought flickering in the front of his mind, before this monumental discussion, that he fervently wanted to see them touch each other. He didn't know why it was important or why the lack of this parental touch came to haunt him, but Tom couldn't recall ever seeing a full embrace between them, much less a fond kiss as he had read of in stories.

Tom recalled his favorite tales of love: despite his supposed disgust, Fitzwilliam Darcy could barely control himself when the Bennett older sisters were in the room. Trotwood, too, expressed a keen joy in merely touching his dear Agnes's gloved fingers surreptitiously. Why would his father not even attempt to brush his hand near his wife's? Tom had no more time to reflect on this observation. His father rose, motioning toward the tall cabinet behind their guest, but Uncle Tim waved him off: "No, I thank you, Sully, but I'll not be drinking or eating for quite some time after that feast our Kitty laid before us on this happy day."

Tom's mother smiled her thanks briefly but said nothing; domesticity was the only forte she was allowed. Knitting rhythmically without seeming to know she held the needles and yarn in her hands, she waited as decades of womanhood had trained her to do. She seemed so old to Tom then, though she had only been in her thirties when they had this talk. Oddly, this would prove to be the longest sustained talk Tom ever had with his parents. Tom, of course, was offered no alcohol; he may be old enough to be allowed in on the adult's evening conversation on this rare and special occasion, but no one in the room even considered performing actions that would give evidence to an actual rise in his stature.

Uncle Tim, never before at a loss for words in Tom's memory, coughed in an obvious attempt to stall, but once he did begin what must have been somewhat rehearsed, it flowed smoothly; he pulled down the power of the remarkable orator he was.

"Katherine, Martin," he began formally, nodding at each in turn, "our Thomas has given us much about which to be proud. God is surely very pleased with him." Uncle Tim smiled at Tom as he paused. Tom shifted at his overt praise. "We can expect great things from him in years to come."

"Thank you, Father Tim," Tom's father said quietly. Despite their lifelong ties of true friendship and even in his own home away from the censor of strangers, Tom's father held Uncle Tim's position in the church in such reverence and perhaps fear as to always reference his ordained title.

Tom's mother nodded without speaking. Looking back on this etched scene in his memory, Tom sensed he hadn't been as astute at discerning all the nuances of the conversation at the time as he hoped he had become, but even then he felt a keen tension and understood several agendas were on the table despite his ignorance of the speakers' intentions. Tom studied his mother busy at her work; she seemed no more taciturn than was her wont; she spoke rarely beyond the confines of her domestic sphere.

Kitty donated her utilitarian baked goods for church festivals as was expected of her; she knitted socks for the wounded veterans; she corrected innumerable childhood squabbles, but she indulged in no gossiping friends or other frivolities. She made no lace and fashioned no ornaments for her daughters to wear. For the first time ever, Tom wondered if she enjoyed anything in their limited circle. Her fleeting glance between stitches was familiar to Tom: stop staring—it's rude. She could chastise any number of infractions silently and had all his life. Without hesitation, he did as commanded, looking instead at Tim who was speaking again.

"And it's our Tom's future I'm wanting to talk with you both about now that we're together and have a moment to reflect on it," Tim spoke these words quickly as Katherine's countenance changed slightly. Tom felt rather than saw it, but she also seemed to shift her weight as if poised to fight off an attack. Her knitting remained rhythmic. If Uncle Tim noticed a flicker, he didn't acknowledge any intention on her part to interrupt. Brushing an errant hair off his forehead, he continued, "I've thought about this for some time, and I'm convinced Tom should further his studies with some educational travel. He should see more of the world than we've been able to show him here."

Stunned doesn't capture Tom's emotional state at this moment. Nothing had prepared him to consider any such wild plan. He wasn't sure where this was going, and suspected his parents didn't either. "What is 'educational travel'?" Tom thought. "Is that what he said?" His mind tried to sort out Tim's unusual words and what they could possibly mean. He felt as if he were walking away from a loud sound in a tunnel and grasped the chair arm in the likely chance he fell as the room reverberated all around him. What was happening? He was going into the seminary; he would be a teacher and a priest. He was already a teacher and a priest; the seminary was merely a formality not yet checked off his list. Wasn't he? No, Tom knew he was still only Tom. But Father Thomas hovered in his peripheral vision. His mother had allowed for no other images to enter his view.

Tom had seen nothing wrong with this idea as he grew up spending weekends cleaning the churchyard instead of playing with classmates, memorizing Latin instead of contemplating the fascinating discoveries surrounding electricity, serving as an altar boy long before he was strong enough to carry the heavy ornamental candles during Mass. He knew nothing else.

To the delight of his maiden aunts and doting mother, from an early age, Tom could recite long passages, not of the Bible, of course, but of the rigid catechism, which to his Catholic family seemed close enough. Rules comforted Tom's mother. From his childish answers of "God created the world" to the complex rationale of Sunday Mass instead of Sabbath worship, through all that the Holy Ghost had and would accomplish, to the recitation of rote prayers of gratitude, supplication, and remorse, he was familiar and adept.

Familiar, yes. But, now, in the drab reality of the only home he had ever known, with the very air awhirl with possibilities and changes, his eventual self watched Tom's movements with a keen and critical eye. This was a step Tom had been poised to take all his life, an irrevocable step, a daunting step, but one he was ready to take. And into this comforting certitude and staid stability, his greatest model was offering alternatives? Why would Uncle Tim do that?

Tim was still talking when Tom could again focus on his strange words: "The fathers at St. Paul's did an admirable job of imparting what limited knowledge can be confined into a rigorous course of secondary education, and now in graduating from St. Christopher's with his teaching credentials, Tom has excelled in all his studies. I am very proud of him."

Tim's fingers reached unnecessarily toward his hair again in a habitual gesture as he continued, "Nonetheless, he needs a wider vision of life to fulfill his potential. He's only just 19 and has his whole life ahead to finalize his vocation. I've arranged for Tom to be granted a scholarship of sorts from the Archdiocese that would cover passage costs and a modest living while he travels perhaps through Ireland and of course onto Rome, if that's the route he chooses. He can stay at the various rectories while he travels. I'd like to ask you, Tom, to consider this idea of mine." Tim stopped speaking, but looked as if he wished he hadn't; the anchor of his words was tangible now, its weight descending on the room, but he felt unmoored. Tim sat rather abruptly on the chair across from Tom's parents.

Tom was unabashedly staring at Uncle Tim. Katherine glared at Tom as if he had somehow coerced Uncle Tim into this preamble for reasons she could not discern.

No one was under any doubt that she had impatiently agreed to a years-long delay she saw little need for when Uncle Tim had ushered Tom into a teaching college to gain his certificates to become an instructor. Uncle Tim had assured her this was an appropriate and wise use of Tom's time and talents. Now, though, her glance lingered long enough for Tom to feel its ominous disapproval when Uncle Tim began his melodic intonation again.

As if in response to Tom's discomfort or Katherine's stare, Uncle Tim turned slightly to her, "Kitty, I realize," he stopped and added, "Sully and Kitty, I realize Tom's immediate future may not be something you've considered."

Katherine could contain herself no longer. Never stopping the needles clicking, she said, "Faith and be glory! Of course we've considered it, Timmy." Of all living people, only Tom's mother called His Excellency, the Most Reverend Timothy Thomas O'Rourke, Archbishop of the Archdiocese of Boston, *Timmy*, and every time she did, Tom's father winced.

Tom didn't wince because he had trouble registering any of the exchange and felt as if he were drowning. "This will be over in a minute," Tom's anxiety spoke in his left ear. "Everything will calm down, and Uncle Tim will announce this was all his idea of a joke. A joke that priests say to each other as they enter the fold. That's it." Even as Tom breathed in this comfort, he recognized the absurdity. Why would anyone toy with such a personal move as this? It wasn't a joke certainly, but then what was it?

Uncle Tim didn't seem to notice any sort of lapsed courtesy. Tom's mother continued, "We've thought of it every hour since the day you baptized him nigh on 20 years ago now. Upon your recommendation but against my better judgment, Thomas has wasted the last two years in secular learning; he could have started the seminary just after he finished at St. Paul's. Not that I'm not proud of his accomplishments; he can surely be a fine teacher as a priest, but he needs now to concentrate on taking his orders. He's set to go to the seminary before the fall chill sets in. You know this as well as I do. It's never been a secret. The boy wants it, so why now do you bring up this...this vision of his potential? That has always been the plan; I've even prepared linens for his travel. He'll be finding his 'wider vision' as you call it within the walls of the Abbey, I'm sure." For a woman little given to long speeches, Katherine spoke to this imposing man who led thousands as if he truly were her flesh and blood brother and they were arguing over a chess board.

"Yes," Tom's now agitated mind nodded as he sat silently with his father as the words of his future flew across the room. Tom began a barely perceptible rocking as he thought: "That's right. I am ready. I have always been ready. Mother has always been ready. I will go into the seminary and into this life and not come back. No one has ever asked if I were not ready. So I must be ready. Of course, I'm ready. Why are they continuing to talk about this?"

Stubborn to a fault, Tom's mother would not help her friend.

"Kitty," Uncle Tim tried again, ignoring Tom's father in earnest now and barely acknowledging Tom's presence in the room, "Tom's a bright lad. We both understand that. But he's a might too young for this decision."

"Too young? Too young for what?" Tom thought. "I don't feel young. I feel...well, I don't feel old, but I'm old *enough*, surely?" Mouth slack, Tom looked back to the match.

The sound Tom's mother made in response was between a laugh and hiss. No one would imagine that she held any animosity toward Uncle Tim, but neither did he intimidate her. That had to be rare in his experience of the world where he unwittingly commanded such awed reverence. She repeated, "Psshhtt," before renewing her move, "Timothy O'Rourke! What nonsense are you talking now?! You were younger by a full year when you left us all for your vocation. What makes you think it has changed so much now only a generation later? Our Thomas is as much a man as ever you were; it's fine he'll be after the homesickness wears thin. When you started this performance, I thought it was something serious you were bringing forward, but now I see not. Go on with your 'he's too young.' Thomas was born old. And it's a fine priest he'll be making just as soon as he goes off to start the process this fall. Besides any of this new-found concern over his age you've conjured, you know we could never pay you for your extravagant offer. Thomas will do best to keep his mind focused on the poverty aspect of his vows. At least we've been able to well prepare him for that."

Tom said nothing. As if a silent pawn slated to be moved across the board dispensable and replaceable, Tom waited to hear the result of this increasingly heated debate as if only mildly concerned. Never the center of attention at least within his hearing, Tom could scarce penetrate the tangle of emotions this conversation created. He secretly wished the tangible tension would last indefinitely to allow him time to savor the attention. Knowing it would not, he strained to stay with the volleys so he could later examine each stroke in his memory.

"She's proud of me," Tom smiled. Of all the points large and small vying for attention of the room, he drew this offhand morsel to his heart willing it to morph into a glowing acknowledgement of him for nothing other than being him. He longed for her to clasp him in an embrace and cry tears of pride and joy on his grateful shoulders. He would go so willingly, so happily into this now-questioned future if only she would hold him as he only vaguely remembered from some point in his child's memory.

Tom's father also said nothing, as was his wont, but he sat stone-faced as if in dread of God casting down retribution for his helpmate's rash behavior and lashing tongue in front of His Holy Eminence. How many times had Sully taken refuge in the certainty of silence in response to his wife's outbursts? Tom seriously doubted his father could have any more ideas ricocheting through his mind than Tom did at that moment. As if father and son were invisible or totally absent, Uncle Tim and Katherine continued to discuss this utterly original alternative for Tom's future in elevated voices. Another rarity in this home.

The noises of Tom's existence were the apologetic clink of pot on burner, the accidental door slam of inconsequential departures, the drone of dialogues no one remembered even as they happened.

These murmurs framed the comings and goings of Tom's everyday. Tom thought of this comforting normalcy. It wasn't no sound; it was simply not this harsh exchange deafening in its oddity. Tom had no doubt his many brothers and sisters were hanging on each word beyond the thin walls; this was too monumental to be ignored even if it were possible. Their own futures a certain drudgery, this debate held sway as a novelty at least. This was no gentle monotony of resigned acceptance. This no diffusion of potential conflict before the embarrassing raw emotion emerged to lopside the forced quiet. Elevated voices presupposed actual feelings, unrehearsed conversations, ideas half formed and timid but never shushed in their infancy to emerge fully grown and uncontrollable.

"You would never need to repay any money. And of course, he's a fine man, Kitty. Surely, it's not the homesickness that concerns me," Uncle Tim spoke as if deliberately knocking her objections off a list. "We all carry a bit of it in our hearts; I know that. It's…not…. He needs more time." Uncle Tim wasn't changing his tack despite Katherine's obvious objections. Tom had never heard such a heated discourse.

"Time for what?" Tom thought again. It never even crossed his mind to join in this conversation so seminal to his future. He'd just wait to see how it concluded much as he had done in Father Etzel's history class reading the antiquated arguments about taxation or land seizures of displaced peoples. Far be it from Tom to expect to have a voice or even question why he didn't. Regardless, this was all so far beyond any previous projection of his life, he could form no words. So he listened to see which side of the revolution he would land on. Tom's silence was not apathy; he longed to speak, if only to note the incongruity of this discussion, but he wore the mantle of unquestioning silence so long familiar.

Uncharacteristically setting her never-finished knitting to the side, Tom's mother concluded: "I won't hear of this." She spoke slowly, moving herself heavily from beside her wilting husband. Uncle Tim also stood to confront his opponent. Kitty dropped her yarn as she stood, and Tom watched it roll across the thinning carpet, suddenly enthralled by how such a haphazard movement fascinated him. A thin green snake traversing the jungle of their threadbare urban lives. It slithered just beyond the scuffed leg of the pompous chair near Tim's left foot. Had he moved a fraction of a space, he would step on it, but he didn't, and Tom was forced to redirect his eyes and thoughts away from the errant mass of yarn so suddenly displaced to the crisis booming around him. Katherine spoke slowly, "You are putting your own prejudices onto our son, and you have no right. No right at all. He is not you, Timmy. And I'll not be having you make him so." Katherine's child-rearing bulk had her panting in this rare posture of unresolved conflict.

"Nor is he you, my dear Katherine," Uncle Tim responded less gently this time.

Calming his frustrated tone, he held up his hand as if in supplication as he slowly said, "Kitty, I never claimed otherwise, and you are the first to know that. Tom needs more time. You're right; I *am* reaching back to my days of decision. What else do I have to offer? I plainly see now I was too young as well, and I should have waited to see what life was about before I became what I am today."

He again worked away some imagined hair from a brow never truly mussed. He continued, "I should have prayed much longer and focused more attentively. I didn't do that, but Tom can. Waiting to listen is not a sin. I'm not saying I wouldn't have become a priest, or that our Tom won't either, but no one was there to guide me, and I swore I'd never allow that to happen again if it were in my power." They stared at each other for so long Tom thought they had forgotten the gist of the interchange. He was wrong, but Tom wasn't the only one uncomfortable in the room.

Tom's thoughts wondered: "'Nor is he *you*,'" Tom silently repeated Uncle Tim's words, savoring their furtive implication. Tom's mind flashed: cold, soft, dark. The room blurred and became somehow foreign. The light ebbed into focus from the edges first. He was still here. He wasn't dreaming. Again the drone of cold and dark.

Tom was jolted back to the scene by the sheer force of his mother's next words. "Well, fortunate it is then this isn't in your power," Katherine was so certain of carrying her point, she visibly relaxed; the threat had passed. Gently now, in the magnanimity the righteous victor can so well afford, almost maternally, Katherine murmured, "I'm sorry you feel you spoke your heart too early, Tim. But I'm sure you're the only person in all of Boston who feels such. You're a fine priest and bishop, dear, dear Timothy. We all know that, and Thomas, *my* Tom, as a Fitzgerald, will follow in your footsteps." Her voice rang with a confidence she had allowed to build incrementally, just as she had prepared her son for this step all his life with deft machinations. Regardless of the wisdom and desires of all the others in the room, she knew in her long-patient mother's heart she was right, and she knew now she had won her point. This discussion was over, and it would become a mere flick in the family history she had so precisely ordained; perhaps she would even laugh at this momentary resistance. Resuming her abandoned needles, she fumbled for her missing yarn without looking, confused at why it was not where she had last left off.

Uncle Tim seemed to make a concerted effort as well; when he spoke, his words were quieter, but still directed mostly at Tom's mother, "Thank you for your approbation, Kitty. You have always been more than kind to me, but I'm afraid it *is* in my power to stop…delay this move. Thomas must wait. I'll not approve his entrance to the seminary now. He can speak to me when he's ready—next year perhaps, or the year after." He turned abruptly away from Katherine.

Katherine looked as if she had been struck; the color drained from her face as her confidence withered. Tom half stood from his place instinctively moving to protect her, but he stopped. No visible stroke severed the connection, but her hold was broken. He knew he stood apart from her now as he knew nothing else. Tom's mother recognized she had lost, yet she couldn't resist hissing as she drew in her breath, "You wouldn't dare." Her unmitigated fury forced Tom's appalled father to emerge from his invisibility.

"Katherine McDermott!" Tom's father spoke more harshly than Tom had ever heard. He demanded, "Control yourself, woman. No wife of mine will be speaking in that tone in my very own house to Bishop O'Rourke. If Father Tim thinks Thomas needs more time in prayerful consideration of such a great decision, then he would know, and we will not be arguing." Sully's vehemence surprised everyone—including himself.

"Thank you, Martin," Uncle Tim nodded toward him but wouldn't look at Katherine who was fuming. The usually silent patriarchy she had so long ruled had spoken with a finality she could not usurp. She rose and left the room without a word; the only instance Tom could recall of such abject social and filial discourtesy on her part as hostess and wife.

Tom was both terrified and thrilled. Scared. Enchanted. Curious. Energized. Hearing for the first time that his future was not the established fact he'd always understood it to be may not have been his only fear, but he dwelt on nothing else as he left the only home he'd ever known after the most intense moments he'd ever felt in the house of his childhood.

2.   Hidden

Thou art my hiding place; thou shalt preserve me from
trouble; thou shalt compass me about with songs of deliverance.

Psalm 32:7

The introduction letter Archbishop O'Rourke provided Tom had impressed him more than once on his exploratory trip. In his haste to depart, Tom hadn't even thought to look at the contents before presenting it, initially expecting a generic, albeit sincerely worded request to provide shelter and a meal if not temporary employment if such were available for him. Of course, Tom should have realized even just Uncle Tim's position and title warranted attention, but, too, he seemed to have connections everywhere, no matter how far Tom roamed. He was almost embarrassed how quickly it turned skeptical half-glares of annoyance into apologetic servitude.

Tom smiled under his newly acquired moustache more than once at the transformation, glad he'd attempted to age his countenance with this helpful addition. The pastor's secretary in St. Louis had almost fallen over her chair: "If I'd just known, Mr. McDermott. We could have prepared the best rooms. They're terribly dusty, they are, Mr. McDermott. I just didn't know that's all. I wished we'd known that's all. You must be so terribly tired, Mr. McDermott." She'd droned on in her limited vocabulary for a few more minutes before Tom assured her a plain bunk would be fine.

Determined as Tom was at the time to be one, he wasn't a priest yet after all, and refused to take advantage of Tim's reputation. Not that most priests realized any sophisticated degree of domestic ease as they engaged in their parochial duties or as they traveled "on business." But the small community of dedicated disciples did usually enjoy a modicum of familial comforts in the homes of other clergy. It was a rather lonely knighthood, a mysterious fraternity of intelligent, well-read men linked by a passionate calling to serve and bound by nearly 2,000 years of purpose and devotion to a Christ-emulating life. This was a private world, away from the constant scrutiny of being a stated role model, and most priests enjoyed the rarity of displaying hospitality in exchange for like-minded company when the opportunity presented itself. Tom enjoyed being a sort of junior partner in the corporation as it were. In the quieter rectories he visited, he could see glimpses of his future in this active but contemplative lifestyle.

Tom determinedly thought if he could only set all the elements surrounding his decision down on paper in a methodical, systematic approach, he'd have this whole issue of his future settled. He would decide, with conviction and the utmost confidence and resolution, of course, announce his decision, and move forward to implement the necessary actions. This pragmatism appealed to his surface nature—clean, neat, efficient.

He made cumbersome lists of all sorts. He enumerated everything he loved about the Catholic church. That was a long list in his romantic youth. Such dedication of purpose; such an unalterable path for life. He lingered fondly over the progression of Mass—the ceremonial parade of regal players robed in bright colors. The thrilling pomp in an otherwise drab existence. He often carried candles or incense, holy water or the crucifix in his mind's eye gliding toward the altar. He was a part of an age-old spectacle of dignified grandeur.

Tom loved to see the entire church rise and fall in synchronization—standing and kneeling on invisible cues; that was his first notion of spirituality as a child. He marveled at how God could command and entice so many people to move together so smoothly as if in a collective trance. That an invisible being could mysteriously achieve this impressed the small boy. Even when Tom came to understand more clearly that the people weren't somehow forced into compliance, he was still impressed by the enormity of the power.

He could close his eyes and hear the cadence of the memorized prayers...hailing Mary, blessing sweet baby Jesus, or entreating the many saints to intercede for poor sinful souls. Even behind closed eyes, the boyish devotee could still see the flickering candles that appeared as dots of light on every available surface around the cavernous church lighting the specific prayer assigned to each flame on its flight to Heaven.

Tom's approval list continued to catalog his young impressions. The priest always seemed so...different...so much more spiritual than the regular people. He stood above and away, arrayed in finery to separate him even more firmly. The berobed priests turned their backs to the mortals and spoke to God in a different language even. As a child that worried Tom, but no one else seemed to mind. He asked his father once if he understood the Latin words, and Sully answered that he knew enough to figure out what he needed to know, which somehow didn't satisfy Tom even then. He later learned he could read along in English on every other page of the worn and musty missal, but Tom himself silently frowned upon that crutch by some self-imposed discipline. That the words and meanings posed a sacred challenge to his young mind and at all times were difficult to decipher translated into a feat somehow spiritually rewarding. Tom felt certain that if he were to become a priest worth his salt, he must know intuitively, beyond a shadow of a doubt, when each *kyrie eleison* sounded and how to anticipate each touch of his breast with no help from a script.

Holding to his synchronized plan, Tom tried to invert his list—what he didn't love about the church he was born into. This part proved more difficult as he knew nothing else. Criticizing the Church was not acceptable behavior at home, so the specter of guilt would push down any negatives quickly in his earliest renditions of the list.

Until Tom was an adult, he had never stepped through the doors of a different denomination's church building, and then only rarely. His parents would never have approved of his curiosity about the way other people worshipped. Most of their friends were Catholic, of course, but the few who were not seemed objects of pity to Tom's parents, and, as such, the children were instructed brusquely to pray *for* them but never *with* them.

Tom thought initially this difficulty indicated he didn't have any items to include on such a list, but that wasn't true. He simply didn't want to commit any misgivings to paper as if he were being disloyal merely by honestly assessing the institution to which he planned to commit his life. Eventually, he was able to generate items for this second list. Some of the very items were the same as from his love list, which made no sense at first. Our likes and dislikes often mirror each other.

For all Tom's awe of the pageantry, the costumes, the scripted scenes, he was uncomfortable wondering if God needed him always to be neatly dressed and impeccably groomed to be in His presence. Tom had no one to ask either. Church was the only destination for which the children were required to bathe and dress in non-utilitarian clothes. God must mandate this ritualistic cleansing if his mother extended so much effort to that end, Tom surmised.

Tom continued listing. The priests seemed to realize the beauty of the promises of hope and love their words claimed in Latin, but very few others listening appeared to be certain, even Tom's own father. But then the parishioners weren't actually listening to the hope and love; they could only hear the beautiful cadence of a familiar, ancient language and left well enough alone without bothering in an attempt to understand the meaning. No one in Tom's childhood realm ever questioned this disconnect, not out loud anyway, so he supposed he shouldn't either. It was enough for the priest to understand what was being said and done—everyone else need only repeat and obey and comply. Never question why. The priest in his God-given authority would translate and interpret and think for the rest. In a communal sense of ownership, if the priest were intelligent and comprehended things his flock did not, then that reflected well on the whole group—they were somehow better and more intelligent vicariously.

Tom's mother's impatient response to one of his earlier questions of this ilk was something along the lines of, "Thomas, when you need to know such things, if God is willing for you to, you will. Until then, recollect yourself and do not embarrass your father or me by asking Father Deene impertinent questions. He's far too busy to explain God to you. And honestly, what's to explain? Be a good boy and be still; it's a mystery. We're not supposed to understand."

As could be expected, he learned quickly not to ask his mother theological questions. He fabricated a theory that he would eventually study all such questions as he prepared for entrance into the priesthood, when as an adult he would be better able to cope with the unraveling of such sacred mysteries.

3.   Waiting

Love is patient, love is kind. It does not envy, it does not boast, it is not proud. 1 Corinthians 13:3-5

Lottie had long before decided she would marry no one but an Irishman – one from County Cork if she could find the image she'd created with such geographic precision, but certainly an Irish husband. According to an indulgent Lottie, it had been only acceptable for her dear Papa to marry her dark-haired French mother because Mamá was so flawlessly beautiful. This loveliness was an indelible image Lottie could only muster from her familiarity with the large portrait hanging in the grand hall. The delicate lace lingering along the deep blue gown flowing down the length of the woman's small frame declared a gentility Lottie never tired of pondering. Beautiful, always smiling, always kindly quiet—forever the perfect woman for a young girl to emulate.

Never having known this saintly foreigner, Lottie sketched a figure now possessed with legendary status for her motherless child. With her child logic, Lottie had long suspected her mother's non-Celtic background had surely led to her early demise. Having ample time on her hands growing up, Lottie created her own personal creation mythology based on her overtly Irish appearance, her deep devotion to her ruddy father, and her infatuation with a motherland she knew scarcely better than she did her own often-blessed portrait mother.

Walking away from the smiling image and crossing herself quickly as if in a self-created church, Lottie mused on the mystery of how her father's blatant Irish-ness had settled on her just as her mother's weaker and vague heritage of some insignificant non-Irish otherness had been usurped by the tiny infant.

Lottie allowed herself to delight in her red hair gently curling down her slim form only as she dressed for the day. She wasn't too vain, just pleased she had the proper coloring for her Irish dream and the ability to manipulate her hair for her own purposes. As a young child, she had adopted the habit of wearing her hair always up in complicated braids and twists as one of her ways of looking older. She had long dressed her own plaits quickly and adeptly. With no mother to sway her to remain more childlike in appearance, decisions of this sort were typically accepted by her hired attendants as innocent enough. She always hoped some unknown ancestor would bless her with more height, but she'd hit five foot five inches at 14 and was becoming resigned to this being her adult height.

Being an adult Irish woman was Lottie's all-consuming mission in life at 18. Having always been the only woman she knew in her father's life, she longed for the age and subsequently the position in his world that would allow her to be more and more important to him as a hostess for the social obligations he had nearly abandoned in recent years. She had never stopped long enough to consider whether he wanted this help or that most daughters moved away from their fathers and into the heart and life of another man at her age. Those images were safely stored away to be retrieved only when her whim deemed appropriate. That she had the County Cork plan for marriage in place was enough. Her version of an idyllic Ireland, the perfect Irish husband eventually, and her safe place by her doting father's side played fancifully in her mind at the slightest provocation. She was submerged in lovely ideas of a land of magic and perpetual green—this easy transfer from the daily routine in Galveston to a land she defined and frequently revised suffused her entire being much as Father O'Mallary's sprinkling of holy water gently washed away her supposed inequities.

"Lovey," called Mary Ellen Kilkenny, the pleasant woman who ran the Gallagher home, "we may be making a ruckus for naught, you know. We've not heard for certain your father's coming home today. He's a very busy man."

Flitting back from her emerald dream, Lottie frowned without ire as she answered her dear surrogate mother, the only adult female she deferred to, "Ah, Mary Ellen, please don't fuss! Papa's coming home tonight for sure. I just know it."

They were moving quickly around the grand mansion the Gallaghers and everyone else in Galveston knew as Cashlin. One of the grandest of Galveston's palatial homes, Cashlin sprawled arrogantly across four oversized lots side by side and front to back. Comfortable as each room was known to be by its visitors, Cashlin was more of a working estate than a simple home really, but it set neatly in with the other less imposing structures just off the busy main thoroughfare in the middle of the bustling city. Cashlin was far enough from the port on one side of the island and the beach on the other to be safely isolated from either, and removed from the financial district sufficiently to maintain a subdued sense of sophisticated elegance. Daniel Charles Gallagher, Lottie's father, had built this colossal structure to impress his young bride from New Orleans. By all accounts, she was a petite regal beauty who looked even tinier and more fragile next to her burly husband, and rumor mongers whispered harshly that rough Danny Gallagher had paid a high price to be accepted by the dainty Genevieve St. Claire. They were both so very young when Daniel brought his darling Ginny to the humid center of his cotton empire. Other businesses certainly prospered in Galveston, but Gallagher's white wonder set the financial standard. With Ginny's beauty and vivacity and Daniel's flowing cash, the young Gallaghers happily pioneered lavish entertainment and created long-relished social events to which the island elite and the nation's privileged coveted invitations.

Daniel and Ginny's sincere generosity soon quieted the rumors and brought true friendships. Cashlin opened its doors to Daniel's many business connections from around the world as well as local leaders who wanted a share of Daniel's far-flung influence. Ginny sparkled on the arm of her proud husband enjoying her role as the social mastermind behind their opulent life. When the Prince of Wales travelled through the East Coast to the adulation of the country, he surprised many by ending his tour in Galveston with a stay at Cashlin to meet Daniel's wife in person.

Not every day was devoted to entertaining royalty and negotiating with capitalist dignitaries. The couple strove to bring all of Galveston a share in their own prosperity. Daniel was always asked to head boards and commissions. He oversaw the creation of the new library as well as a retirement home for sailors. Ginny quietly led teams of church ladies at St. Patrick's to care for the elderly and shut-ins. They donated the seed money to build the St. Mary's Orphanage the Sisters of Charity of the Incarnate Word needed to carry out their mission, and coerced their rich friends to follow suit.

Always doing; always giving. Much of that trickled down to Lottie as she grew into her life's role. Before her birth, her parents' personal joy was elevated to a fever pitch when Galveston heralded the news that a son was born to the beautiful couple.

Patrick Daniel, the darling of his parents' hearts, was a chubby baby just tottering on his unsteady feet when tiny Ginny was expecting another child. Friends and associates approved of this rapid expansion of the empire that seemed to have every advantage. Cashlin would be the boisterous, happy home of a passel of children set to inherit not only wealth and social standing, but also their place as genuine favorites among the islanders.

But Charlotte Elaine would be Ginny's last expression of love for her young husband. Ginny died quietly in her room after a long struggle to bring her daughter to life. Daniel defied convention and the wishes of the attending physician to be with Ginny during the ordeal that wrenched happiness from him and changed his life forever, his only consolation being that she had his hand to hold as she left this world. It had been so sudden, so utterly violent for Daniel that he went into a sort of shock for years. Still so very young, and now alone with two motherless children, Daniel only maintained the sanity he did to preserve these miniatures of his beautiful wife in their innocence. Their rearing he entrusted entirely to Mary Ellen, the one servant who was more like family, having been so long in the fold. The children would never want, but his heart ached for his loss, and he gave over his children to others. He recovered his spirits enough to continue on in his business life, but he no longer brought people into his grand home. He stodgily kept up his established cotton trade, maintaining his position as a leader in that industry, and took some small, distracted joy in seeing his handsome children in their youthful progress, but Daniel without Ginny by his side little resembled the man who took Galveston by storm first by his business savvy and then by introducing his enchanting, exotic wife into the social scene.

Lottie knew bits and pieces of this tragic tale, begging Mary Ellen to repeat the familiar scenes whenever she could finagle a story from her busy guardian. The fragments formed a lovely fairy tale mosaic in Lottie's mind as she longed for the embrace of a mother she had never kissed and the undivided attention of a father she could not quite captivate through the sad memories she evoked for him. She dedicated her life from a very young age to making her father happy and proud. Patrick had grown into a somewhat sullen young man who seemed bored with life despite his unlimited resources. He wasn't a bad sort; he loved his sister dearly and respected his father's wishes dutifully.

At 20, Patrick had left Galveston to discover what he wanted to make of himself as his father had noted on his departure. As if awakening abruptly upon Patrick's completion of school, Daniel realized his son was little like he had been at 19, already a husband and well on his way to being one of the richest, most influential people in the country. Perhaps feeling some guilt, Daniel hoped travel and a bit of contrived responsibility in exploring the various elements of Daniel's business would help Patrick overcome the absence of a stronger guiding father during his childhood. Patrick was a good boy, but he would need help to become a good man. Sending him away was the only help Daniel knew how to give.

"Well, Lottie, my dear," Mary Ellen continued as she placed the last of the goblets down on the starched white cloth, "please don't be terribly disappointed then if he becomes tied up in his work again. Love you as he surely does, Darling, Mr. Daniel is a very, very important man and has much more to consider than coming home to the likes of us, I'll be wagering."

"I'll be able to talk him into staying longer this time, Mary Ellen, I'm sure of it," Lottie claimed as she inched forks into a more perfect alignment with the glimmering china set for four at the table.

Mary Ellen looked up, satisfied with her work, asking, "Who are our guests, Dear? I don't recall you mentioning Maggie would dine with you today."

Lottie's brow creased as she pouted, "I do wish it were Maggie or MariLyn, Mary Ellen. They are both far and away of more value to me than that peevish Mr. Morgan and Artie. I had no choice really or I would have found a way to avoid having them again. But Papa seems to enjoy the old man's company, so I wanted it to be pleasant on his first day home."

"That's rather harsh, Pet. And you really should act more kindly to young Artemus, Lottie," Mary Ellen gently scolded her ward, "I suppose he's been in love with you since the two of you celebrated your first communion together, and you could do worse than to have such a gentleman by your side."

"You're right, of course, about my choice of words, and I am sorry Mr. Morgan provokes me so; I must work on holding my tongue. But what nonsense you talk about Artie, Mary Ellen. Stop it at once or I'll leave!" Lottie flushed at what she imagined was likely true and upset her more as time passed by because she realized her silence on the subject seemed more to encourage young Artemus than to discourage.

"He isn't so bad, Lottie," Mary Ellen continued. "You should be his friend; you've known Artie all your life."

"Exactly!" Lottie began pacing as she answered, "Perhaps that's the problem. He *is* my friend, but how could I possibly…what? Marry him? Or even…even love him…knowing him so well? He might as well be my brother since then at least we could be comfortable around each other. I'd as likely fall in love with Patrick or Father Liam for Heaven's sake!"

Mary Ellen's tone took on none of Lottie's excitement as she drawled, "Well, I daresay by the looks of it, Artie doesn't share your wish to make you his sibling, but he'll make someone a decent enough husband and sooner rather than later is my guess, Dear One. I wouldn't be totally disregarding his advances if I were you until you have time to think of all the advantages he could offer you."

"Mary Ellen! How can you go on so seriously about such utter balderdash!" Lottie flushed at her friend's chosen topic, recalling how often she'd unwillingly been thinking in this same vein recently. "What possible advantages could I enjoy without...what could he offer me that would mean more than...oh, Mary Ellen, why would I ever settle for a life with a man like Artie, a man I haven't even an outside chance of loving the way I must love a husband? I'd rather go without a husband if that's the only alternative."

"And what way would that be, Lottie, that poor Artie can't quite measure up?" She had moved to dusting the ornaments in the adjoining parlor, her petulant mistress mindlessly following her through her housekeeping duties. Mary Ellen's tone was loving and gentle but serious with a growing concern she'd tried to temper recently with timely advice to this child, who was as like her own as if she had given her life in addition to her motherly love all these years. "Methinks, my darling, you've buried your head too long in your fancifully stories," she ended playfully.

"Well, what's wrong with turning to my books for guidance, Mary Ellen?" Lottie tried to sound stern but couldn't quite pull it off. "Do you seriously think Lizzie Bennett would look twice at Artie? And poor, wonderful Jane gave up all pretense of self-preservation to stay committed to her true love even when she could not be with Rochester. She would have easily walked straight away from my tragic hero without a second glance!"

"I know, I know," Mary Ellen rose to her feet and continued dusting, "I've read them all, too, remember? But don't you think they all seem rather…too dramatic? Forget about those story girls. What would make *you* truly happy, Lottie?"

"I guess I don't sit around and think about that too much really, Mary Ellen," Lottie winced at her lie. "I'd like to be like other girls and plan all the details out and worry about the color of my dress and which side my hat's feather needs to be perched on this week, but then I get so bored. Anyway, the man I want to marry wouldn't care about all that. I've never met the kind of man I'd want my husband to be. I've read that some people think he doesn't exist – that he can't exist the way we have things set up now, but I don't believe that. Father Liam says I'll know when God sends him to me. We'll just have to set things up a little differently for my ideal to exist, I suppose." She smiled at Mary Ellen who encouraged her with an expectant look to continue. "Oh, all right. I see you'll never let me rest until I tell you my version of the man who will make me the happiest of women."

"You're right," Mary Ellen concurred, "but then my girl has always been so bright. Do tell."

"Well, for starters, I just can't believe God would force me into something so serious as a lifetime of marriage without letting me know beforehand that it is absolutely right. No, I know God will let me know. I don't think God forces anyone, but people just get so desperate to see what they think they want to see and don't stop to consider what they are doing. If they just waited a little to listen....Oh, I know, I know; I'm not telling you my secret plans! You're incorrigible! Let's see, my husband, of course will be handsome to me even if not exactly so to everyone else; that will make it easier to keep him to myself! But really, he'll have to know without me telling him why I have to be the way I am even when I'm so different from other people, and they don't like the way I'm being. He'll want to help me be different like that without waiting to be asked and without making a show of it as if he were receiving points for his behavior in some sort of tally. And I'll be the same for him. The purpose of our lives will become honing the means by which we help each other be happy and productive and able to help other people. He *is* out there, Mary Ellen; I know deep down he is. We'll just go together like it says about the two becoming one—only it will *really* be that way, not just a pretty thing to say at church." Lottie stared out the big window through the lace.

"My, but that sounds like a tall order, Angel! Your picture is very pretty indeed, but who will be able to live up to that?" Mary Ellen's teasing tone became more serious as she said, "Your fancy talk is all well and good, Dear, but it isn't wrong to remember that Artemus Morgan would be able to keep you," Mary Ellen paused and held up a delicate porcelain dancing figurine she had been moving to dust the table, "...in this manner."

Suddenly more intent than before, Lottie said, "True. I'm sure you're right about the money and all. Oh, I know you'll laugh, Mary Ellen, and I probably don't even know what I'm saying, but I don't have to have this." She looked wistfully around at the incredibly beautiful room with its soft rugs and shining surfaces. The imported chairs that created the perfect balance between style and comfort, their very number belying any notion of economy or thrift in this household. The vast draperies falling gracefully from the high etched ceiling to the gleaming wooden floor specifically designed to mark a drastic difference between the reality of the street so close outside and the protected aura of the haven inside this room making each seem a faraway continent when in one or the other. Lottie had known nothing else—this was her only world. And yet she claimed to wait for a love for which she willingly would turn her back on this opulence and security perhaps forever.

Mary Ellen smiled kindly at her favorite wondering if Lottie's literary notions of true love and devotion would actually survive in a less impressive environment. She spoke quietly, "No, Lass, you're right. This…," sweeping her hand around the grand room, "this is not what love is about, but it can make your life easier when the pain comes. And I've never seen love without pain lurking nearby, sad as that may sound."

"That's just like Mama and Papa, isn't it, Mary Ellen?" Lottie spoke the names reverently as one mentions saints. "They were so happy. But then so sad….Is that what love has to be though?"

"No, no, sweet one," Mary Ellen tried to lighten her tone, "love is happy and bright, and it isn't something you have to figure out or worry about either. It just is. You will know when you've found it, just as our dear Father Liam told you, so we won't be sitting idle anymore today to discover what your perfect man will be. Just pray, 'St. Anne, St. Anne, please bring me a man!' That's what we sang when I was a wee one in school anyway." Her strategy paid off, and Lottie happily went on her way with a smiling face; the only factor diminishing her joyful anticipation of her father's return was determining how best to endure an evening not encouraging her ardent admirer.

As it turned out, dinner that night was not the happy homecoming Lottie had hoped to make it. Her father's work kept him in Baytown—again, he'd wired late in the afternoon. Robert had brought her the telegram himself knowing she would be disappointed. Diligently hiding her disappointment even from herself, Lottie was sorely dismayed at her father's busy schedule that seemed to keep him away from Galveston as much as it took him from her when he was in town, but she was mostly vexed at having to play hostess to the Morgans alone. Daniel's long, unexplained absences from home hurt. Lottie loved to care for him and mitigate the worry the business world imposed on him, and she missed his society. They talked of books and music, and he told her of his travels. She tried valiantly not to complain when he was away so often and kept herself busy with friends and projects knowing no request of hers would be denied by her father.

On this occasion, she decided while Robert was still in the room to remedy that annoyance immediately.

She would take her sour situation and try to sweeten it enough to endure the taste.

Lottie typically didn't stay angry or upset long; it took too much energy. She simply maneuvered negative situations around to be as pleasant as possible for herself and those with her; that was her gift. It was far too late in the day to cancel the engagement gracefully, so she extended her hospitality to others in her desire to be surrounded by detractors to Artie's possible machinations. She quickly wrote out dinner invitations from her neat stack of gild-edged cards to her dear friend Maggie and to Father O'Mallary and Father Liam Rooney, her pastor and her lifelong friend, respectively, and told Robert to wait for replies. She then hurried to find Mary Ellen to readjust the menus to accommodate the extra diners. Cashlin rarely received rejections to invitations, even impromptu ones, and adding another few places caused little stir with Sarah, the Gallagher's long-time cook, but Lottie knew better than to risk any surprises with her staff and went down to the kitchen to compliment and cajole, soothing any anxiety caused by additional guests.

Lottie walked away from the kitchen slowly, secure in knowing the meal would be a brilliant success at least. As she wandered to her room finishing the cookie Sarah had thrust into her hands as she hurried her mistress out of the busy kitchen as Sarah had done all her life, Lottie wondered if she were being perverse, just arguing with Mary Ellen against a match with Artie for the sake of arguing. Regardless of her very real aversion to the typical feminine pastimes of shopping for finery and contemplating dress patterns, Lottie understood the social climate as well as any other woman her age. She had more resources, a quicker mind, an indulgent father, and a long-absent mother to mark her individuality when set against other women coming of age. But she fully understood her options in society. As much as she may wish it to be otherwise, she knew she could stay living with her father single for only a few years more before she would be considered eccentric and thus less attractive to eligible and respectable suitors.

Artie Morgan was certainly respectable and indubitably eligible; he stood to inherit all of his father's considerable fortune, lands, and many businesses. The Morgans were another of Galveston's many success stories. And Lottie admitted, her childhood friend was more pleasant by far than his father who made even the simplest social engagements awkward and tiresome. Her father's respect for Mr. Morgan and their well-established friendship based on their similar perspectives on commercial aspirations and Mr.

Morgan's impressive business acumen in whatever operation he dabbled kept Lottie respectful and compliant in her conduct toward the Morgan family.

Perhaps Mary Ellen was right, Lottie had mused more than once regarding this very topic. Artie wouldn't be an odious man to live with. He was courteous and certainly attentive—overly so really. Almost as if protecting Lottie was his over-arching object in life. It was sometimes unsettling to be such a project. But he was kind to Lottie, and they had known each other all through their childhood. By dint of sheer familiarity, Artie counted as one of her more rational choices for potential suitors. She kept up this see-saw of attributes and wondered why she felt dejected sitting at the emotional bottom of the scales when Artie's real qualities as a possible mate surely outweighed any of her flimsy detractions. She could never quite muster the ability to convince herself that loving Artie—as a husband, not a friend—was her destiny. That was not God's promise of a soul mate as Liam had patiently explained it to her.

4.　　Favor

Go, eat your food with gladness, and drink your wine
with a joyful heart, for it is now that God favors what you do.

Ecclesiastes 9:6-8

Her ploy to fill the dining room with chatter worked admirably well, and Lottie was pleased with herself despite longing to see her father. She did love her ability to entertain and lavished attention on her guests. Father O'Mallary, as usual, was grateful for being included in the social invitation, and Lottie never questioned what he seemed to feel was his right to her hospitality, but her favorite spiritual advisor never incurred a sense of obligation on her, and she invited Father Liam as often as possible. He was a true friend and unusual in her limited experience with religious leaders. All others she had known had acted so sad and almost angry, probably because they were all so very much older, she surmised. They didn't seem to believe the joyous words they preached about how much Jesus loved everyone; rather, she thought they focused so much on the onerous seriousness of one's duty and the evils lurking everywhere waiting for careless sinners that the joy was pushed away and relegated to the next life. But Father Liam was different. For one, he didn't act as though he knew all the answers, although he certainly could hold his own and was intelligent when the after-dinner discussion floated to theological inquiries. He also wasn't from an entirely different generation. Lottie wasn't sure how old Father Liam was, but knew in most priestly circles he would be considered young, and ironically good looking.

Father Liam's greatest gift to Lottie was his unabashed joy of life. He was a good friend to her, and they were comfortable in each other's company. He showed her, mostly through example, but sometimes in serious discussions, that being happy was more than just acceptable to God. According to Father Liam, all creatures were ordained to be happy and optimistic and hopeful. This was Father Liam's definition of faith.

"Because, Lottie, my friend," Liam had once explained, "if the faithful aren't joyful and grateful, what does that say about our trust in God and all the promises He has made?" The question had stuck with Lottie ever since. With this guidance, if nothing else, Lottie had permission to hope in an unassailable faith in God's unknown plans for her. With such similar driving forces, Father Liam and Lottie were fast friends.

Liam thanked Lottie for the steaming coffee she handed him and said quietly to her only, "I do hope we'll be celebrating the Bard's birthday again with you, Lottie. The children loved that day so last year. I have been so mired in meetings for the new school building of late, I haven't heard any plans yet."

Lottie's eye lit up with enthusiasm at the change of topic from the rising cost of shipping cotton across the waterways she'd been forced to contemplate by her proximity to the father and son Morgans. "Oh yes, Father," she offered up eagerly. "I was just putting the last of the details together for that project this week. I think we'll do much the same as we did last year. Do you think the children will mind?"

"Mind? I think if you changed even one tiny insignificant trifle of that dream for them, they would cry foul," Father Liam smiled at her excitement. "What a grand time it was, too. Are we to have the ponies again this year? I think that was my favorite part."

She laughed remembering, "Unless, of course, your favorite was the ice cream Sarah concocted—you ate five bowls if you had a spoonful!"

"That was for the ponies!" Liam laughed heartily at their shared memories.

The previous year for her birthday, Lottie had made what her father first felt was an odd request until he saw how genuinely happy this present made her. She wanted to throw a party at Cashlin, but instead of inviting her then 17-year-old friends to an opulent dress ball or a formal dinner, Lottie wanted to bring the 90 some odd children and 10 nuns from St. Mary's Orphans Asylum for a celebration on the lawns of the mansion. After making sure this was really what Lottie wanted when she could have had absolutely anything in the world, Daniel had laughed and given in, allowing her free rein. She had loved every detail.

She brought in strolling singers, pony rides, kites, hoops, tops, lemonade, and, of course, ice cream and cake. Each child left with two gifts: a small toy and a small book; for many, they were the first presents they had ever received, and they treasured the emotion-filled novelty as well as the baubles. Lottie's friends came and played games with the children and acted in skits and scenes they had taken from Shakespeare's plays and poems with Lottie at the lead. She planned it on Shakespeare's birthday, April 23, which happened to be hers as well, a twist of calendaring fate about which she was always very pleased. Lottie treasured the birthday memories from this party more than any of her previous years' celebration extravaganzas. She had been so happy seeing the children running around the yard squealing with delight. The children's infectious joy fluttered her heart, but Lottie had been almost as pleased watching the usually staunch sisters actually laughing. The image of Sister Mary Agnes leaping in the air to divert an errant hoop and stick would bring tears to Lottie's eyes for the rest of her life, she was sure. The intended two hours of organized play beautifully lazed into an entire afternoon of radiant fun for children who had so few lovely memories such as this day provided on which to cling. By evening, exhausted from running, playing, and for once eating their full of the ordinary food and delicacies never remotely imitated at St. Mary's, the children willingly prepared to return to reality with gratitude and love shining out of their tired faces.

Lottie smiled at her dinner guests as she came out of her memory of last year's revelry and said, "Let's do make a note, someone, that the ponies we find for the children must enjoy ice cream!" The others within hearing laughed with genuine enthusiasm, remembering what an event the day had become. Some neighbors had appealed to Lottie's father to reconsider the size of the party. One man on her father's board of directors actually suggested Lottie be allowed only to invite ten of the very best behaved orphans to avoid the noise and bother of controlling so many; the others could enjoy vicariously. Lottie had laughed out loud at the idea with her father when he retold how the man had been serious. Spending significant time helping the sisters, Lottie knew the children at the orphanage personally and could never have singled out any of them; her father indulged her many requests for whatever Lottie decided the children needed.

Artie was the first to speak with a tone of seriousness that sounded strange in the glow of the previous banter. "Miss Charlotte," he looked down as soon as Lottie turned at the mention of her name, "I could bring my...I mean, I'm sure my father would be willing to allow me to bring up some of our ponies for your party. We have a small ranch on the other side of the island, you know. Father, you don't mind do you?"

Mr. Morgan and Father O'Mallary had been discussing other matters while the younger people plotted Lottie's party. He looked up distracted, "What is that, Artemus? I wasn't paying attention to anything but my talk with the good Father here."

"I said," Artie repeated, "we would be happy to supply the ponies Miss Gallagher needs for the afternoon of her birthday party for the orphans. I could bring them myself."

"We have servants for tasks such as delivering livestock, son. Do try to recall that please. Surely you have more important tasks to command your attention. Why would you need a pony for a party, Miss Gallagher?"

Lottie tried to hide her smile, "They eat all the ice cream, evidently."

Father Liam laughed with her but looking at Mr. Morgan's bewildered expression decided to intervene, "Miss Gallagher does incredible charitable work here on the island, Mr. Morgan. She is planning to repeat last year's fabulous success when she invited the children from St. Mary's to a party here at Cashlin on her birthday in April. We need ponies for the children to ride."

"I see," Mr. Morgan said, but it was evident he didn't. Mr. Morgan saw the gaiety on the faces of the others, although he realized his son seemed to hover on the edge of the planning, which slightly disappointed him. "Father, no doubt Miss Gallagher is well respected among her class and familiar set, but I question the decorum of thrusting the practices of one class onto the inadequate shoulders of lesser beings; do the foundlings actually have any way of acquiring appropriate attire or bringing a suitable remembrance for such an affair?"

"Oh, no, Mr. Morgan," Lottie exclaimed, flushing, "I would never ask the children to attend a function that would embarrass them or remind of them of their unfortunate situation in life."

Father Liam took up Lottie's explanation, "No, Mr. Morgan. I didn't realize you were not in attendance last year. Miss Gallagher created a special party for the children themselves—all 90 of them! It was Miss

Gallagher's birthday, but the children received the gifts and the food and the flutter of attention, which is something too few people think to give them. Children without parents are reminded constantly that they have no one to be responsible for them and to pay attention only to them out of pure love as children with parents do. For one afternoon, the children from St. Mary's forgot that distinction last year and loved the party, and Miss Gallagher has generously planned a repeat performance."

Father O'Mallary produced an audible interruption somewhere between a cough and a growl, which was the subconscious way he typically directed others to pay attention to him as he spoke. All eyes moved to his face. "Miss Gallagher, your father's munificence is known all over Galveston and far beyond. He and your beloved mother always gave generously to suitable charitable endeavors under my suggestions. That your father indulges you in this type of frivolous outpouring is, I fear, the recklessness of a doting parent unrestrained by the calming influence of his dear, departed helpmate. You, My Dear, certainly cannot be blamed for that weakness. Regardless, I think we can all determine a far more…responsible means of distributing these valuable resources more efficiently. I see this as God's wise intervention into our feeble actions, actually. Mr. Morgan here is a fine business man, and he and I were just discussing the needs of the poor in the parish before you brought our attention to your notion of wasting vast sums on a transient flash on the lives of so few, who already have all their physical and spiritual needs met at the asylum. We must not spoil them and have them expect more from life than will be their eventual lot. It only makes it more difficult on them, you see, and I daresay that was never your intent. Gentlemen, what should we suggest to Miss Gallagher's father upon his return to make a better return on his generous contribution?"

Hoping she had been able to mask the shocked disbelief on her face as she listened to her pastor drone on, Lottie choked down the rising anger in her throat before speaking, "Father O'Mallary, I appreciate your attention to such a trivial matter, I'm sure. But my father has already made his decision; we make a rather small fiscal committee, I confess, but he has placed all bursar responsibilities with me on this project. And, with all due respect, Father, I am convinced in my heart that the children do benefit greatly from this simple show of love. They need festive whimsy and spontaneous recreation every bit as much as they need warm socks and porridge, Father. They must have joys and memories to anticipate and hopes for the future.

All of their young lives cannot be discipline and privation. Where else will they generate a sense of creativity or a generous nature for themselves? We have some very intelligent children at St. Mary's, Father, and the sisters do their best, but they are almost overwhelmed. I love helping in this way."

"But you must see, my Dear," Father O'Mallary droned again undaunted, "we will be able to spend the money far more wisely for the needs God has placed before us."

Father Liam diplomatically interrupted before Lottie could answer, "I agree with Miss Gallagher, Father. The children respond very well to this event. And as she said, this is how her father wishes to spend the funds, so I believe our role is merely to praise God for touching the hearts of such generous benefactors and accept the blessings as eagerly as the children receive their cake. Now, Artie, how many ponies are you able to spare? What did we have last year, Miss Gallagher, five or six?" And so the conversation diverted to this vein with only a few mumblings from the older priest as the evening drew to a safe close.

5.   Preparation

Righteousness goes before him and prepares the way for his steps. Psalms 85:12-13

True to his word, Father Liam convinced Father O'Mallary that Lottie *would* spend her money how she wanted, so further opposition was futile. Soon thereafter, the second annual party at Cashlin for the orphanage children became an unlikely social focus for the St. Patrick's congregation and for much of the rest of the island. Everyone wanted to be included; it was the event not to be missed. Lottie had to start refusing some self-invitees just for lack of space, which was telling in itself because the lawns at Cashlin would accommodate hundreds easily. She promised the disappointed social climbers she would come up with another opportunity for them to help with the orphans, wondering if she could persuade them to become truly involved eventually without the lure of such a high-profile gathering, but she wanted to maintain a bit of the intimacy of the previous year's festivities.

Despite this vow, even Lottie acknowledged sheepishly she was going a bit overboard this year when she explained to Father Liam she had learned a small traveling circus would be going through the surrounding area at just the exact day, so she had "invited" them to stop and entertain the children. She quickly mentioned the need for a taller temporary fence around the garden wall as Liam laughed at her retreating figure after Mass one Sunday morning.

"A circus, Lottie? A real circus? What are you doing?" Father Liam smiled at her enthusiasm.

She looked at him cautiously, but then saw his smile and knew she would prevail, "Liam, it's a *very* small group really. 'Circus' is actually overstating the ensemble. And anyway, how many of these children will have the opportunity to see an elephant again? Just think of it! What are the chances a circus of all things would be in Dickinson just the day before our party?"

"Only you could have such favorable odds, I'm sure, Lottie! God *always* takes your side. But an *elephant?*" Father Liam laughed. "Poor Robert will have a fit—do you have any idea what an elephant will do to that lawn of his?"

Lottie smiled at the image, "Oh, it's only just a baby! Even so, the children can ride him. And Robert can get the grass to grow again, I'm sure; it can be his new challenge! Can't you just see their faces?!"

"I'm trying *not* to see Robert's! So this is why we need the added fence?" Father Liam asked pragmatically, undaunted by the announcement of the elephant.

"Oh, no," Lottie continued in a business-like voice, "the elephant is fine; as I said, he's just a baby, Liam, but evidently, the peacocks *can* jump even if they can't fly, so we'll just need a little wire mesh over the front gates. The rest of the wall fence is sufficient."

"You act as though this is such a normal request, Lottie," Father Liam smiled at his friend. "Seeing as how we mustn't encourage even dainty elephants and jumping peacocks to run amuck in the streets of Galveston, I feel obligated as your spiritual leader to find some way to help! In fact, I'll send our new handyman to you later this afternoon if that would be soon enough. His name is Tom, and he's very nice. He's helping Father O'Mallary tidy up after Mass, and I think he plans to head down to St. Mary's after our noon meal."

"You are always so kind to me, Liam," Lottie smiled as she began walking away. "Thanks. I'll be sure you get to ride the elephant, too."

***

Tom had not met Lottie at this point, and frankly, it was difficult for him to remember much from his thoughts BL—Before Lottie, as Father Liam would later tease.

Tom was physically very close to William as Lottie ran into his life raving. It's not an image many could forget easily, and one Tom would never even try to lose. But Tom didn't exaggerate in the least to say Lottie lost her mind momentarily in her concern for the boy. Her temporary insanity was as charmingly beautiful to Tom as every other state of mind she expressed. Her maternal nature touched him, and Tom was smitten immediately.

Later the same day Lottie spoke to Father Liam about her party plans, she checked on her father, who had fallen asleep over his newspaper after lunch and went into the grounds looking for any loose ends she might need to attend to before the party at the end of the week. She was happily familiar with the gardens and outbuildings of the estate. The staff took no offense at her gracious interference; often she actually lent a true helping hand with the flowers and fruit gardens; she knew what she was doing and didn't shy away from hard work. Turning the corner of the house and thinking about the roses that would delight her in the next few months, the sight that caught her eyes terrified her. She realized she was trying to breathe and pray and scream simultaneously when she was finally able to shout as she began running toward the boy who was dangling from the edge of the roof corner too high to avoid injury when he fell. She gasped out, "William, hang on. I'll fetch help. Please hold on."

William was surprised to see Lottie running and tried to hear what she was saying because she looked upset. The idea had flashed through his mind for an instant that maybe she was hurt, he later said, but she was running faster than anyone hurt would be able to. He'd never seen her this way, but he knew something was wrong. The group was just far enough away from the main house that her screaming would likely not rouse anyone inside. William waved at Lottie from his perch on the ladder, and started to swing around to climb down, but that seemed to agitate her even more. What was she saying?

"No, William. No! Just hold on." Lottie screamed even louder now and coming up to Tom and William, "I'll run back and find someone to help me get you down, but you'll have to hold on until then." She stopped abruptly as she reached the cause of her concern and realized the image that had worried her so from across the large expanse was wrong; she didn't quite understand why it wasn't as she had suspected it, but she realized William wasn't dangling from the roof after all. He was somewhat precariously standing at the top of the old ladder leaning to reach a long wire on the side of the gatehouse, but he seemed totally unconcerned for his safety. He actually was in no danger at all. By the time she ascertained her erroneous conjecture, she was standing at the bottom of the ladders, flushed and panting.

Lottie was still visibly shaken by what she had supposed as she snapped, "William Stuart DeHaven, you come down from there this instant!" The now-frightened boy responded immediately and scrambled down not knowing what he had done to excite this wrath.

Then she looked up to the ladder next to William—Tom's ladder. Angry as she was, Tom still couldn't help but be mesmerized by her energy. It wasn't just that Lottie was arguably the most beautiful woman he had ever seen. But she was also the most passionate person he could remember ever encountering. The range of emotions passing through her face in these few minutes was fascinating; what incredible power for such a tiny thing. She was full of life and responded equally to the fear, concern, anger, and then relief as she realized her young friend was not in immediate danger. How could William not feel the love of her relief? Tom wondered if she always had this impact on people or only in emergencies. Looking up into William's young face and unapologetically crying grateful tears, Lottie was hugging the very confused, gangly teen firmly as she turned to look up at Tom, still flushed with the sensational combination of exertion and emotion. Her skin visibly sparkled in the sun as she attempted to compose herself and control her breathing.

Wiping away her tears, she turned her attention to Tom, "And you?! What exactly do you mean, Sir, to place this child in such a dangerous position? How dare you! He could have fallen to his death! I've never seen such reckless irresponsibility. Honestly! Please explain yourself." She must have realized that her projections were slightly exaggerated since the "child" towered over her by a full head and was obviously unharmed unless he were at risk from excessive blushing over her attention. But Tom scrambled down from the ladder just as quickly as his young partner had moments before jealously knowing he would not receive the same reception.

William, now understanding her mistake and seeing the passion in her still-flashing eyes, tried to defend Tom through his embarrassment, "Oh, Miss Lottie, I'm not hurt any. Please don't cry. And don't be mad at Mr. Tom. See?" He quickly moved his arms and legs in an awkward pantomime as proof of his well being, smiling shyly. He explained, "Father Liam sent us over here. We weren't trying to do nothing wrong; honest. Mr. Tom and me were just fixing your fence for the party."

"'Mr. Tom and I' and 'anything wrong,' Dear," she corrected automatically, smiling finally in relief. "Thank you, William, for explaining the situation to me."

By this time, Tom had come down the ladder with his hat in his hand, almost as embarrassed to speak to this beauty as William had been, but also compelled by her frank smile to move forward, Tom said, "Miss Gallagher, I presume? I'm so very sorry for frightening you. Father Liam indicated we could just do this work without disturbing you about it. And William was securely on the ladder the entire time. I was holding it steady at the top; your angle must have obscured the image. He was connecting the wires across the gate opening."

"Well, I was indeed frightened," Lottie said. "William appeared just to swing there in the air as I came from the house. I couldn't understand how he could help but fall; I seem to have overreacted a bit, I see now. Forgive me; William is a favorite of mine." Setting off a renewed wave of confusion from the bewildered teen, Lottie looked fondly at the boy she must have known well. Tom sensed even then it wasn't lost on her how truly close in age they were and that his limited prospects and drab life could so easily have been hers but for mysterious twists of God's grace. She turned to him still smiling. "Whatever would I do if you were to hurt yourself, Wills?"

Tom contemplated the exquisite gift she gave this lonely orphan that afternoon by casting her full attention toward William with such genuine maternal concern for his safety. Tom would learn that this is Lottie's special gift. She gave to others that which they most needed.

Blushing wildly, William stammered, "I...I won't, Miss Lottie, I promise I won't. I'll just run put Mr. Robert's ladder back in the shed; I think we were done anyway. I'll be right back, Mr. Tom." Making fleeting eye contact, William ran off to escape any further embarrassment.

Lottie turned to face Tom fully now looking distressed at her recent outburst. "Please do forgive me. I'm afraid I've not made a very nice first impression, Mr. Tom—I don't even know your name; I'm sorry. I have an uncanny way of running away with myself and creating scenes, I fear."

"Thomas McDermott, ma'am," he said quickly. "The children at St. Mary's seem to like Mr. Tom better. And please don't think of this again, Miss Gallagher. The fault is entirely mine; I thought we could make the barrier a bit more aesthetically pleasing than to mar the beauty of the front entrance with mesh, so I proposed to William that we try this; I think it will suffice. I should have notified you that we were here. William was so excited when I asked him to come with me, and I can see why." Tom spoke in a rush and realized too late he was making a fool of himself rambling, hoping to prolong the minutes with Lottie. An observer might have thought Tom were some freak who had never seen a woman before.

Tom noted with surprised relief that Lottie didn't seem to think his ramblings wild. Her voice was musical when she spoke, "Well, Mr. McDermott, William is such a wonderful child—young man really. He'll go on to build great things one day, I project," Lottie warmed to her topic again as easily as she had flashed with emotion earlier, but her recent anger was gone. "And, thank you, Mr. McDermott, for your assistance here. When Father Liam mentioned sending someone to help with my project this morning I'd expected one of the workers from the church."

"You're correct," Tom smiled broadly. "I'm the new hired help, although I'm sure I'm not near qualified enough, and Father Liam treats me more like family. I've been…well, moving about for a while now trying to decide where I'm supposed to end up, I guess. Father Liam and I have been trading travel stories and book notes well into the night since I arrived. I've only been here since about the first of the year, Miss Gallagher."

"Oh, you are fortunate indeed to be able to spend time in conversation with Father Liam. I unapologetically attempt to monopolize him at every opportunity, which unfortunately is never enough for my taste. He is one of the kindest and best of men," Lottie enthused. "I don't suppose the good Father mentioned to anyone sane such as yourself why you were sent on this mission this afternoon though?" She had smiled at her own nonsense.

Picking up her tone, Tom spoke with mock formality, "Actually, Miss Gallagher, I was under the distinct impression Galveston may soon be overrun by errant, fence-hopping peacocks and delicate elephants bent on destroying manicured lawns, but beyond that I have and need no details. All in a day's work." She laughed gaily at Tom's response, which was reward enough for risking being such an idiot. Tom tried to keep from staring at her, but couldn't be sure he was succeeding. They were walking back toward the huge house that seemed more like a castle from Tom's experience of residences and chatting easily about the upcoming party for the children.

Lottie seemed totally at ease with their casual discussion. She asked, "Where did your journey begin, Mr. McDermott?"

"My family is from Boston, Miss Gallagher."

"Ah, Boston," she replied wistfully, "I've always wanted to see the old cities on the East Coast. I love to travel; mostly though I only get to go places in my books. Every once in a while, Papa has allowed me to accompany him on his business trips, but I've seen so little really. We had plans to travel to Chicago together for the Fair, but that fell through. We did have a lovely adventure in Washington and Virginia a few years ago, though. I had such fun in all the beautiful museums and monuments."

"I travel by page pretty often myself. I've never been to Washington, but I want to," Tom said, knowing he wanted nothing at this moment so ardently than to continue this wonderful, comfortable conversation.

"And you are simply wandering now" looking off a bit, Lottie made it a statement not a question. "How absolutely delightful!"

"It has been interesting at least," Tom answered.

"I find I enjoy myself far more when I allow myself to float more than stay exactly on course," she said as she looked down at the path in front of them. "I'm afraid my character is a bit more of a straight-line follower than a floater though, so I have to work hard at getting off track. I love to play and fret and worry over the details."

She smiled so sweetly that Tom ventured, "I'm usually more strict with precise plans myself as well. But this journey is a little bit different. And, so say the leprechauns anyway, one does meet the most fascinating people just off the beaten path."

"Communing with the wee folk, are you? Is Galveston your rainbow's end, Mr. Thomas McDermott?" she asked playfully.

"Perhaps it is, Miss Charlotte Gallagher; perhaps it is," Tom answered.

After mentally questioning the wisdom of speaking to strangers of mythical creatures, Tom wondered why he hadn't been more forthright with this beautiful stranger about what he was truly in Galveston to find. Tom had never kept his eventual vocation from anyone before. Was that technically lying? During the months of his transient existence Tom had prayed and thought seriously about where this journey would take him, knowing even his staunchest of supporters would expect an answer soon. His mother's persistent letters all contained this theme lightly disguised as news about home and the family's goings on.

All Tom could ever come up with was a nagging uncertainty he couldn't explain well even to himself, but that he could easily dismiss for days at a time by dint of hard work and full immersion into whatever pressing project his host priests needed his assistance on. Tom liked service, but had known that about himself even as a child. Life change could wait, he had assure myself.

Until that very day, Tom supposed vaguely he would end the uncertainty by returning to Boston to enter the seminary as his mother had always planned, having obediently and willing given Uncle Tim this second delay in his pilgrimage toward my long-settled future. Everyone had doubts, didn't they? Tom wasn't so unusual. When he did focus his wandering mind on the reasons for his quest, he would inwardly debate the merits of foreign mission work, teaching in rural areas, a medical vocation of some sort, or even a scholarly route such as Uncle Tim had modeled heading into the hierarchy of the church itself.

Tom often spoke with the priests he lived with about their opinions; they all had suggestions and warnings—some more emphatic than others. Never once in his ramblings had these thoughts ever turned to determining some way he could remain in the church without becoming a priest. Standing in the extensive gardens of Cashlin with the estate's charming heiress shifted Tom's perspective on a lifetime of thinking and planning and wondering.

Without defining his motives or analyzing his present actions, for the first time in his life, Tom was immensely pleased, albeit still confused, by the fact that he hadn't finalized his decision. And yet even these distracting thoughts could take no definite shape in his mind because they were so alien to his imagination. Tom was a million miles away, and his world was upside down. Tom only knew he was glad he was standing where he was at this moment. He needed no other conditions met.

As William and Tom bade their hostess farewell, the look of amused gratitude she flashed at Tom made up for any memory of rebuke in her voice before. Lottie had made a new friend, and she was pleased. As the men stepped to the iron gate of the side entrance to the estate, Lottie said, "William, thank you. And I am terribly glad you didn't fall off a ladder today. And thank you so much, too, Mr. McDermott. Please do your utmost best to forget my ridiculous behavior earlier. I do hope you'll come with Wills and Father Liam and the children to our little party. I'll look forward to seeing you again."

6.   Party

They will celebrate your abundant goodness and joyfully sing of your righteousness. Psalm 145:6-8

Walking in the beautiful gardens of Cashlin had rarely been the sensory overload it was on the day of Lottie's much-anticipated party for the children from the orphanage. The black-gowned sisters filed the orderly children through the gates in their best clothes, starched and ironed vigorously, ill disguising the worn seams and thinning elbows of the garments repeatedly handed down from one inmate to another. The façade of calm structure dissolved the moment Lottie smiled and announced composedly that all the adults were at their disposal and the children were to play with everything they could see, eat until they were full, and share nicely, but otherwise cavort to their hearts' content. Unsure exactly what *cavort* meant and not willing to miss a chance at this glorious and rare escape from routine, a few of the older boys made a dash for the food tables piled high with childhood delicacies, and the melee ensued.

Slightly worried that Lottie's offhand invitation had been mere courtesy, Tom repeatedly asked Father Liam if by coming along he would be intruding. "Actually," Father Liam smiled, "Galveston's most charming hostess asked after you in particular when we spoke last after Mass. She seemed intent that you be there."

Tom needed little encouragement for an opportunity to see Lottie again, so accompanied the priest. In fact, Tom had thought of little else for the days since their first meeting. The children were already becoming a favorite element of Tom's assumed responsibilities in the parish. So many of them! It reminded Tom on a grand scale of growing up with so many brothers, sisters, and cousins. How would they all turn out? Where would they go? Each with a story waiting to be told.

Liam wasn't content to sit for long with Father O'Mallary in the shade where Lottie had directed him to a low lounge chair, asking one of the children to bring the old priest a plate of food and a cold drink. Father O'Mallary enjoyed being treated majestically and rested easily in this pampered role to oversee the festivities from his retired position, just as Lottie had planned, no doubt.

Father Liam and Tom moved among groups of children and watched their eyes as they listened to the young actors performing sword fights and dances. Squeals of delight punctuated the air as the children spied the elephant, such an exotic creature to their minds and so huge even in his babyhood. The awe was palpable. The children seemed perfectly at ease despite their wonder at all the out-of-the-ordinary elements of this day.

Miss Lottie was their beloved Fairy Queen, and only she could have created this magic. Whenever Lottie arrived at the orphanage, the children quickly realized, they ate better, had more supplies, and sang more songs than on other days. Miss Lottie, they knew, was the reason the sisters frequently allowed the children to visit the beach and the tall ships, and she always figured out a way to turn any trip away from their school into a picnic or some other treat.

The children had long ago appropriated Lottie as their own, just as they understood the sisters were surrogate mothers in a strange dance of church-sanctioned emotional adoption. The women strictly forbidden to create but duty-bound to nurture did so with a maternal zeal that could only be intuitive.

Lottie was positively glowing in her contented approval of the day's event. She spoke familiarly with the nuns and her many friends who seemed to be as enthusiastic as her young guests at their part in the party. Lottie moved from cluster to cluster and was always welcomed with a touch or a hug or a smile as she called the children by name, joined in their play, and introduced her old friends to new friends. Several of her father's associates were in attendance as well, and Lottie made the rounds to these groups as if she were a polished social manipulator.

Coming from reading to a group of the youngest partiers as they moved on to another treat, with a colorful book still in her hands, Lottie waved heartily from across the lawn as she spotted Father Liam and Tom walking toward her. Tom felt a pulse pass through his body as if he'd been physically shocked as the group drew together.

"Miss Gallagher," Tom spoke first, "you have a tremendous success on your hands. I am truly grateful to have been included. Thank you. This is simply amazing!"

"Ah, Mr. McDermott," she beamed, "the pleasure is all mine." She politely kissed Father Liam's cheek and continued, "Any friend of Father Liam's will always be mine. I'm so very glad you both came." She looked around approvingly, "Aren't the children beautiful? They're so happy! But now to business: Have you tasted everything? I'll have no peace until Sarah hears how you enjoyed every bite."

Liam said, "Please send my immediate regards to Sarah for her cookies and cakes—simply delightful! And Mary Ellen and Robert as well—they make this all look so easy! I *am* glad we were able to pull you away from your storytelling for a few minutes. I wanted you to tell Tom some of your thoughts on the school idea we've discussed. He and I were talking a bit about it a few nights ago looking over the plans. He's incredibly polite to me even when I begin to drone on about our pet projects. He's studied the work Madam Montessori conducted in Italy I mentioned to you last spring. You'll be fascinated."

"Do you *know* Dr. Montessori?" Lottie asked quickly, obviously excited about this subject.

"No, no," Tom admitted throwing his hands up in defense. "I can only claim a novice's interest in such a brave experiment. I haven't even really *studied* the subject, I fear. She is fascinating though—so little support, but her strides will stand the test of time, I'll warrant." Tom focused intently to not lose this incredible opportunity to monopolize Lottie in a setting where she was surrounded by devoted followers all eager for her attention.

Pausing only slightly as she nodded in interest, Tom continued, "I've only read a few articles covering her remarkable work with the children she found wasting away in the bowels of Rome. As I understand it, she's making remarkable headway and garnering not a little interest across Europe with essentially cast off children no one else would even attempt. Think what she could do with children who weren't suffering so to begin with. Her ideas just seem so commonsensical."

Lottie was watching Tom's face closely, which made it difficult for him to stay mentally in the slums of Italy. But Lottie asked Tom's opinion so charmingly, he forced himself to exert considerable energy on the task at hand simply to keep her asking questions.

"She appears to let the children learn on their own instead of actually *teaching* in the sense we know it, doesn't she?" Lottie asked, clearly not feigning interest out of courtesy.

Tom replied, warming to the topic, "That's what I gather from the articles I've read. Her method is very interesting to me, but I admit I don't see how that will produce measurable results beyond the very youngest of children. Are we to allow children, uneducated children at that, to decide our course of studies? Would anyone study mathematics on their own volition?"

Lottie made a delightful sound as she quietly laughed, "True! They might *help* us decide though. To be perfectly honest, left to my own devices, I would know a great deal about tea rituals and manners around an English estate half a century ago from my favorite novels and little else, but, seriously, I do think I may have wandered into mathematics and design on my own when I needed to know measurements for my garden or for cooking with the correct proportions. Sarah recalculates constantly when I haphazardly increase dinner parties. I'm sure she learned rudimentary sums in a school setting, but the rest has been in the kitchen. And she's brilliant there."

Father Liam joined in as excited as Tom and Lottie were about the potential for reaching more children. As the three discussed educational alternatives bringing up questions and new ideas, Lottie motioned to the gaiety around her and asked Father Liam and Tom, "Why can't there be more days like today for them in a school setting? They learn as much about sharing and patience here as they do in a stuffy classroom with rows and desks."

"Not to mention all they can learn about African wildlife," Father Liam mentioned with a grin.

"Or the mathematics they can execute determining the jumping height of native peacocks," Tom added quickly.

"Fine," Lottie tried to make her tone scornful but laughed before she could go on, "I know I'll never live down that adorable elephant or the leaping peacocks, but do look how Emily is laughing at Charlie and how Davy keeps chasing that ridiculous bird! And anyway, I believe Mr. Carter said Penelope was an

Asian elephant, so perhaps we should start with geography when we get settled into our new outside school, gentlemen!"

"Penelope, is it?" Tom asked, enjoying the easy rapport, "Are you on a first-name basis with many other elephant friends?"

At that moment, Daniel Gallagher walked up and took his daughter's hand in his own, saying, "Charlotte, my love, it does my heart such good to hear you laugh! What joy you bring to these children." Turning, he greeted Father Liam warmly as befitted an old friend and looking at Tom kindly but without recognition, said kindly, "Sir, we've not met, I believe, but you keep the best of company, and I'm sure I welcome you heartily."

Lottie smiled at her father, "Oh, Papa. How terribly rude of me. This is Father Liam's friend, Mr. Thomas McDermott. He's staying at the rectory presently and helped us set up for the children's party."

"Sir," Tom began, suddenly more nervous than usual in meeting strangers, "I appreciate your incredible hospitality, Mr. Gallagher. You are a fine example of a cheerful giver."

"Ah, I can take no credit for this show that's for certain. This is all due to Charlotte, Mr. McDermott." Daniel's pride came through in his voice. "She is our brightest light and best example. I'm sure our good Lord is very pleased with her. This is Lottie's idea of her own birthday party, but the presents all go to the children."

"Papa," Lottie blushed charmingly, "you stop now. We were just discussing the possibility of a new type of school. Join us; we'd love to hear your ideas. School is a sort of business, you know."

"Charlotte, my darling little worker bee, even during a party, you talk reform! Well if anyone can change the way children learn, it will be you," Daniel said smiling as he shook his head, retaining his daughter's hand.

Father Liam took up the thread of Lottie's pet subject, "I agree with Lottie, and you, of course, Daniel, know how tenacious she can be once she grabs hold of an idea. Her present plan is to create a more creative forum for the teaching of our children. I am certainly intrigued by the notion, but as Tom just said, I too question the application benefiting any but the youngest of children and that only in social skills, not in true academic subjects. I daresay I've done scant research into these new methods compared to Lottie and Tom. Lottie seems to think we could make learning more like today's events than that to which the children are accustomed."

Daniel smiled, "Charlotte, is this the work you dragged me to New Orleans with you for? To see that Mrs. Kristin Thompson about? Wasn't that her name? That wasn't even a real school, was it? She had gathered up all those street urchins in more of a care facility than a real school. Those children were a bit backward if I recall. They were cleaning and preparing food the day we visited. It was all very interesting in a different sort of way, but is it truly viable for everyday use?"

"Well," Lottie said seriously, "Yes. Some of Mrs. Thompson's charges have brain challenges, but I'm afraid most of their problems stem from neglect and ill use by the very people who should have cared most about them. How could a child possibly focus on division and parsing sentences with the sting of cruel treatment still echoing in his mind? Or hungry? Or tired? Or frightened? I don't know for certain, of course, but I do sense Dr. Montessori's and Mrs. Thompson's work is far more structured than it appears to be on the surface. They work with what you're calling *real* academic subjects, certainly, but they treat them as part of the child's whole life, not just a portion relegated to a school building. And I have no intention of turning every day into a party, I assure you, but...."

Regaining the momentum the discussion had reached before Daniel had stopped for introductions,

Tom chimed in, "No, I see the merit in an alternative to our current system. In general terms, we're failing miserably now. Most children simply do not grasp near as much information and knowledge as they have the potential to learn. My parish in Boston was a bit more successful at keeping bodies in seats than I saw as I travelled through rural area. But to what end if the child doesn't understand half the instruction? I believe Miss Gallagher hopes to establish something more along the lines of Miss Temple's benevolence as opposed to the inefficient treachery of Mr. Brocklehurst."

"Exactly! Of course you *would* know Miss Brontë," Lottie exclaimed, nodding with what Tom hoped was approval.

"Ah, our other favorite Charlotte," Father Liam announced smiling. "Weak as it may seem, I will openly admit that I cried and refused to finish Mrs. Gaskell's biography for three weeks knowing Charlotte would die at the end; such a lovely genius." The group all laughed at Father Liam's admission, but Tom noticed Lottie nodded in understanding as well, which made the couple smile at each other.

Grasping for a topic to change the conversation back to a less personal one after the shared glance, Lottie spoke to her father again, "Well, Papa, can you blame me that I so relish this time? Look at the children! But even more than that I am so thrilled with all the adults—so engaged with these poor children. Lavishing this attention on them; loving them so. That's the real success. I'm convinced this is the only force that will ever change the world. Why, just look at old Mr. Moody—he's actually smiling! That may be a first. Father Liam, have you ever seen that?" She paused only slightly in her enthusiastic description of the scene around us. "The boys love to watch him make those paper boats. He so rarely goes out anymore, but look at the fun he's having. And who knew our dashing Colonel Gresham would help the girls learn fencing with his own sword from Gettysburg?"

Father Liam smiled, nodding, "MariLyn Gresham can convince her father to do absolutely anything, I'd wager."

"She *is* rather persuasive," Lottie continued in raptures at the camaraderie in the air. "Before you know it, she'll convince someone important to allow women to vote—then you better watch out! That's her current project." She laughed as she thought of her friend's political motives that seeped into her every conversation and brightly colored her personality.

Father Liam nodded, "I imagine MariLyn is converting some of the older girls from St. Mary's into her plans for a brighter future now as they thrust and parry."

Tom, too, looked across the yard and laughed, "Actually, I believe that's Miss Gresham converting Penelope with a group of giggling girls watching in delight at the moment."

"No child feels the sting of his lot today," Father Liam smiled.

Daniel joined in the laughter, but brought the discussion back to his daughter's previous train of thought, "And why shouldn't women vote, Lottie love? Watching what you do here! You ladies should run things more. It would be far more pleasant for me to discuss taxes and trade regulations with the likes of you and MariLyn Gresham than it is with the gruff old saws in office now."

Father Liam exclaimed with a grin, "Why Daniel, you sound like a suffragist! You should join us at the Parish Hall Tuesday evenings as we discuss all the programs the good ladies of Galveston already do run."

Tom wondered if Father Liam were being facetious, asking, "Is there actually such a group?"

Lottie and Father Liam exchanged smiles and she answered, "Actually, there is, Doubting Thomas! We usually just go about our business without rocking the island's boat so to speak, but we do indeed execute excellent work. Island beautification, projects for the orphans at St. Mary's, the Seaman's retirement hospital—we touch quite a few if only quietly. Join us this week if you'd like."

Lottie's eyes held Tom's for just a moment as he tried to assimilate all the images flashing through his mind—beautiful, articulate, powerful, generous, altruistic, intelligent. Her voice brought Tom back to the discussion. "You should join us as well, Papa. We'll get ahead much more quickly and much more easily with the backing of several key men in Galveston's power structure. You know I'm right on that score."

Daniel smiled at his daughter knowing he likely would do whatever Lottie asked of him, but quipped, "But Charlotte, darling, you already have our good Father Liam, which must mean God approves. And I'm sure Mr. McDermott and a few of your other suitors would be far better company than your weary, old father."

Lottie seemed flustered at the turn her father's off-hand remarks took, so Tom attempted to distract her father as he wondered if ever he could be her true suitor and not just in jest. "Mr. Gallagher," Tom said after a moment, "Galveston does seem poised on a point of change. Would the business community here welcome women into its ranks?"

Daniel looked at Tom closely as if studying a glass for hairline cracks but only for a fraction of a second, then allowed his face to ease back into a smile, "Well, son, if women do," he looked up at Lottie's manufactured cough and smiled, "*when*...I meant to say *when* women do join the ranks of commerce, it will have to be in a thriving economy such as Galveston enjoys. There's absolutely no reason to resist it. I'm convinced within myself that God's abundance is what allows us to live so harmoniously on this little stretch of land with Germans, Blacks, Irish, and Mexicans already. We don't contend with any of that nonsense causing such grief in so many other places. We just get down to work and go about our business. No one seems much bothered with focusing on minute differences when we have so much profitable business to conduct."

Father Liam interjected, "I'll have to agree, having so many overt blessings does seem to encourage people here in Galveston to a nobler generosity than I've seen elsewhere. Businessmen have no time to suffer fools or join in with others jealous of another's prosperity if all prosper alike. As if God's commandments aren't enough of a reason, it would be bad business to exclude and separate people on a whim."

"Which of course means," Lottie added to bring her point back around, "there's plenty of pie for the women of Galveston to enjoy positions of authority for the improvement of so many causes."

"Yes, yes," Daniel laughed, "and speaking of pie, I must snag at least a tiny slice of Sarah's rhubarb for myself before it all disappears."

Daniel made his congenial farewells all around to move on to business associates of his who had escorted favored daughters to Lottie's fete with just such hopes of gaining a few minutes of Daniel's time, leaving the reformers to continue plans for new and improved educational opportunities. The small group, too, soon broke off to attend to the whims of the honored guests, but not without Tom and Lottie both filing away several thoughts and looks and questions for further reflection in the more guarded cover of later solitude.

7.   Altered Perspectives

Religion clean and undefiled before God and the Father,
is this: to visit the fatherless and widows in their tribulation: and
to keep one's self unspotted from this world. James 1:27

Dr. Paul Bruce looked out toward the water from the desk by the window of his small office. He had only just set up his dentistry practice in Galveston last year, confounding his father and a number of his concerned professors by moving across the country from the plains of Indiana. Some days Paul wondered why he'd done it right along with his father. He'd graduated high enough in his class of newly minted doctors from the Indiana Dental College that he could have practiced anywhere, but he'd wanted to go away from what he knew—away from the cold, away from the city, away from burrowing down into the claustrophobic routine his father so cherished. Meat loaf every Wednesday; a pint on Saturday night; then roast, potatoes, and greens every Sunday after Mass without fail, without question, without exception. The repetition was not a comfort to Paul as it obviously was to his father and mother; the monotony drove him wild.

Paul loved his parents as well as his younger sister and brother, but he longed for change. A late-night session studying for exams captivated his attention when a classmate mentioned an advertisement from the railroad newspaper encouraging entrepreneurial young professionals to move west. Galveston wasn't named in this particular flyer, but soon Paul sought these types of ads and determined to save as much of his scant spending money to take advantage of the promised adventure, prosperity, and mostly the blessed change one of the unknown destinations would afford him.

He enjoyed his practice of mostly poorer families from the neighborhood around his office. Every day he encountered some new challenge that sent him eagerly to his treasured books of dental science, the one luxury he'd allowed himself to bring with him from his former home. Slowly he was teaching his reluctant patients what he knew about their ignored teeth. It hadn't been too long since dentistry consisted merely of tooth extraction performed crudely by the village barber or druggist, whichever had the stronger stomach. Perfectly sound teeth were routinely pulled for lack of more reasonable alternatives in desperate attempts to ease immediate pain. What an incredible waste! Anyone who had suffered that ignoble practice was understandably a hard sell, but Paul had a soothing demeanor and realized he would need to build trust to convince people his services were not a luxury but a necessity.

By dint of hard work and studied sacrifice, he supported himself well enough and dreamed of one day moving his practice closer to Broadway and downtown to gain the more prestigious clientele residing in the mansions he admired on his Sunday walks home after Mass. For now, his tidy office sufficed with its shining white tooth sign proclaiming in glistening gold letters:

Dr. Paul C. Bruce

Practitioner of Dental Sciences

He boarded in a small room at the top of a large old home near the office that had once been much grander, but now served as a respectable, if slightly shabby, place to sleep and take meals. Mrs. Kennedy, the proprietress, was a kind old woman who clucked over her numerous boarders as the mother hen she had been for most of her 65 years.

The dental office occupied the ground floor of a compact frame building directly across the street from and facing the shore. The second story held Upper Crust, the popular bakery now run by Mrs. Joan Coverdale, the young widow who owned and managed the busy shop becoming a professional baker by default when her husband died suddenly, leaving her with few options other than to maintain the business to continue to feed her four small children.

Paul liked Mrs. Coverdale and even enjoyed the antics of her brood. He had a standing order for bread twice a week, and pleased himself to no end when he thought to provide a cookie jar in his outer office for patients to enjoy after their visits; that allowed him to purchase even more wares from the bakery on a consistent basis.

He realized he took great pleasure in being able to help the diminutive Mrs. Coverdale with ordinary tasks when he noticed she was overwhelmed, which seemed to be rather often, but far less than it would have been had he tried to accomplish all the work she did in a day, Paul mused. How could he possibly keep up with so many children! Once meeting on their shared stoop, he told her, "I actually owe you a great deal of thanks for driving patients my way with all the sugar you feed them." Paul remembered that being the first time he'd heard her rich laugh. He'd liked the sound and had wanted to continue their merriment, but one of the tow-headed children—having scant dealings with youngsters, he could never quite tell them apart other than knowing two were girls and two boys, although he assumed they were different ages—called down for his mother, and the laughter ended in a good-natured sigh. Idle moments being so few, they rarely met by accident, and Paul had sat at his desk more than once as he did now contemplating some way to fabricate such an intentional *accident.*

Unable to invent anything plausible that wouldn't seem grossly contrived and thus embarrassingly transparent, Paul determined perhaps he didn't need to work so hard to disguise his admiration for the woman who lived and worked above his practice. He wasn't sure exactly how long Mrs. Coverdale had been a widow, but it had been her status ever since he'd been in Galveston for almost a year. She was young, despite her many children, and very pretty. Surely there would be no impropriety in asking her to join him in an outing. Moments such as these made him long to be able to speak to his mother or sister. He didn't quite want to commit the questions to paper in his regular letters home, but if he had been with them in person, he could casually ask one of them what would be the right thing to do in this situation. If only they would overcome their keen aversion to change and install a telephone. Paul didn't have one in the office yet, mostly to save on the cost, but he knew the telephone office downtown had lines set up for public use. He gathered his fragile, non-female-advised ego and his wavering nerve when he contemplated what to do. Long years of solitary study had left Paul with little time for socializing despite his mother's gentle admonitions. At the time, he hadn't minded devoting himself to learning all he could about his medical field; any sacrifice he made was self-imposed and accepted, but he longed now for some personal connection he couldn't quite define for himself.

One Saturday afternoon, as he bade his last patient farewell, Paul walked up the narrow stairs outside his entrance leading to the bakery's public entrance with determination and confidence. He noticed how clean the landing was kept despite the step-worn stairs and the well-used patina on the banister.

Knocking on the door, he instantly felt nervous and foolish, silently admonishing his thoughtless action, realizing no one would be expecting a knock at a retail establishment, and that he would look the lovesick fool. The family lived in the back of the small shop he knew, but Paul wondered how they managed even the most rudimentary functions in such tight quarters with so many people. Unsure what protocol expected in this situation, Paul was about to knock again and then walk in when the door was moved away from his outstretched fist from the inside. Quickly dropping his hand, Paul smiled down at a delightfully disheveled girl only about three feet tall with an interesting mixture of flour and red jam on her hands and face.

"Oh," the tiny girl exclaimed, trying to wipe her face with the back of her hand, succeeding only in smearing the jam into a pinkish paste on her chin. Looking somewhat frightened, she turned and called into the empty bakery, "it's Dr. Paul."

Paul shifted his weight, trying not to laugh. He remained waiting to be invited into the small shop anyone else on the island would simply have walked into expecting to be served. His mission so ill-defined and his welcome so atypical, Paul lacked the perspective to realize he should act more like a customer and less like an honorary guest.

"Hello," he said quietly to his young hostess. He was about to ask to speak with Mrs. Coverdale when the child at the door burst into sudden and seemingly violent tears.

"Mama's not here," she sobbed.

Startled, but trying not to panic in the midst of this totally alien environment, Paul kneeled to the child's level as another similar-looking child came into view around the screen leading into the family quarters. Paul looked at both children with wonder and asked, "But what's wrong? Don't cry. Maybe I can help you."

The boy who had come in second was followed closely by a taller girl, but all of them looked to be under ten certainly. The girl who had answered the door spoke first in a rush, "Oh, Dr. Paul, I'm Laura, and this is Michael, and she's Katie," pointing to each in turn before she continued on. "And we've made a huge mess. Mama will be so cross when she gets home but she did say we could make some cookies before she left. She had to go to church with Brian—he's our brother. He's the oldest. I'm older than Michael even though he's taller—that's just because he's a boy— Mama told me so. And anyway, I'll have a growth spurt and then he won't be taller than me but I'm not sure when that will happen. I hope it's soon though. Do you know?"

As Laura paused for breath Paul assumed, he smiled at her pace and haphazard subject matter and started to ask when their mother could be expected home when the older girl—*Kathy, wasn't it?* Paul thought—picked up the thread.

Seeming to understand her social responsibilities as the oldest daughter, Katie began, "Dr. Paul, we would invite you in for some tea, but we have to clean up before Mama gets home. If you want a tart or some of the rolls you usually get, I'm sure Mama wouldn't mind you just taking them."

"Maybe I could help you clean up first," Paul said, looking at the three anxious faces obviously concerned at their dilemma between the expectations to be courteous to a guest and customer and their need to remedy whatever mess lay beyond the screen as quickly as possible.

"Oh, could you?" Laura smiled sincerely for the first time.

"I told the girls not to use the big jam pot," Michael spoke man to man. "It's too heavy and now lots of the jam is on the counter. We should have stuck with the raisins—that was my idea. They're in a bag on a lower shelf, so it was a better plan."

"Mama said we could make thumbprint cookies," Katie defended herself. "Raisins would look stupid in thumbprint cookies because they wouldn't stick and would just fall out the minute you bit into one. Don't be dumb. You just like raisins in everything. That's stupid."

As if now beyond any timidity in his presence, the children quickly ushered Paul beyond the faded folding screen that covered the entrance to the living quarters. Most of the room was kitchen, which made sense to Paul since this served the family and the bakery; as he surveyed the small but efficient workspaces, oven, shelves, and supply cases, he felt comfortable and impressed with Mrs. Coverdale's ingenuity. Baking utensils, bowls, cooking pots, and baking sheets stood neatly in cleverly fashioned racks that appeared to be built for those specific items. The appreciative glance took only a few seconds, and Paul agreed with a low whistle that the kitchen area had what he supposed was an uncharacteristically unkempt look.

Michael looked as if he would defend himself again against charges of stupidity, but turned instead to relate, "Mother had to take Brian to learn how to be an altar server. He's 12, and when I'm 10, I can go, too. Father Liam told me so. And Miss Sheryl said in Sunday school that if I learned all my lessons properly, I could make one of the best altar servers at St. Patrick's. But girls can't ever. Even though Katie's 10, she can't go. Just boys."

"That's stupid, too," Katie interjected, moving a pile of spilled flour into a long line on the counter. This must be an old argument, Paul surmised.

"Is not," Michael replied, "it's the law. It's even in the Bible; God said it."

"It is not," Katie shot back on the verge of tears at this thought. The mere threat of another child's tears spurred Paul into action.

"Well, I would think that a candidate to be the best altar server at St. Pat's and the other three of us could have this place back in shape in a snap—long before Brian and your mother return. Want to try?"

Smiles replaced fear-induced and anger-supported tears as all three children set to sweeping and wiping with little encouragement needed from Paul. They quite clearly were familiar with actual work, not just manufactured tasks to keep them out of the way and occupied. Paul helped Katie maneuver the heavy jam pot back into place and helped scoop up flour from the work table. Katie helped Laura make the needed thumbprints into the unbaked cookies and even allowed her brother to help move the cookies from baking sheet to cooling rack despite his earlier heinous comments on gender inequality.

Chatting amicably, the children entertained Paul with stories of their school days and asked him about teeth, his spinning chair, and all the tools they had seen lined up on the shelves in his office. Michael asked Paul what it felt like to put his fingers in someone else's mouth.

Paul laughed and replied, "Well. A lot like putting your fingers in your own mouth, I suppose." Automatically, all four did just that, which made them all laugh around their wet fingers. Paul launched into a description of all their teeth as they looked into each others mouths to see the differences. Having moved to sit on the wide steps leading from the ground floor to the bakery as cooler than the oven-heated shop, the new friends were in danger of succumbing to another fit of giggles as Mrs. Coverdale stopped with one foot on the bottom step with a bemused look on her exercise-flushed face.

"Uh-oh. What have we here, little ones?" She smiled at her three youngest children. "I do hope the children weren't too loud, Dr. Bruce."

Trying to wipe his wet fingers on his pants discretely and trying to stop laughing, Paul stood up from his place at the top of the stairs, "No, no, Mrs. Coverdale. We've only been visiting. We were…." He paused seeing the worried faces of his new comrades. "We were discussing religion, women's rights, and the precise location of the bicuspid molar."

As if his cover story were immensely humorous, the three relaxed into delightful peals of renewed laughter that seemed contagious as even Brian and Mrs. Coverdale joined in, apparently for no other reason than to be included in such gaiety.

Recalling his former purpose in mounting the stairs hours earlier, he mentally rearranged his initial plan and said, "One of my patients reminded me there is to be a concert outside at the Garten Verein tomorrow after Mass. I thought perhaps we could go together."

Something in Mrs. Coverdale's face made Paul think she was about to decline, as he realized he might not have been as specific as he'd intended. "All of you," he added looking at the children's expectant faces, with what he supposed was as hopeful a look on his own face.

"Oh, Mama," Katie squealed, "can we go, Mama? Please. It's so pretty there. Please?"

"Kathryn," Mrs. Coverdale gently chided but didn't sound angry as she looked at the eager faces all around her as if waiting for some monumental decision to be made.

She found herself laughing softly as she said, "The majority seems to vote *yes*. Are you quite certain you're up to this motley gang, Dr. Bruce?" She looked at Paul as if wondering if he would flinch at this inescapable albeit willing and cherished barrier to her heart.

"Absolutely," Paul answered immediately. "We're already 'ever the best of friends' as Pip says." And he realized he meant it. He'd grown accustomed to the children being a significant part of who Mrs. Coverdale was. And not merely from his afternoon with the youngest ones. Somehow over his time working so near the group, they had slipped into his life, and it pleased him as he realized he was not exasperated with what would indubitably be the challenge of courting their mother.

8.   Reflection

So I reflected on all this and concluded that the righteous and the wise and what they do are in God's hands, but no man knows whether love or hate awaits him. Ecclesiastes 9:1-3

On the night of the orphan's party at Cashlin, Tom settled down with Father Liam in his study. They both balanced books on their laps and held wine glasses, fondly recalling the day's events. Father Liam's suite of rooms in the rectory was on the second floor at the back of the old house. His sleeping area was a small, sparse chamber to the side of this room furnished only with a small bed in the corner and a wooden crucifix on the wall, but the sitting room was a comfortable size with three walls of bookshelves filled with hundreds of volumes ranging from poetry to classics to the latest novels of the day as well as ancient philosophy, comic drama, medieval masonry, and theological texts from various religions around the world. Tom loved that these volumes were certainly not decorative. The well worn spines were evidence of the functionality of this room.

Liam's desk was littered with the remnants of his many parochial projects; correspondence, paperwork, and opened books seemed to cover every inch of the surface in inexplicable piles simultaneously suggesting intense productivity and abject chaos. The final wall was nearly all windows set around a stone fireplace producing both light and heat as well as cool gulf breezes by night. The window wall had a small projecting balcony that curved gracefully from the corner of the room with just enough space to stand comfortably outside and watch the water on the nearby shoreline.

Tom looked toward the water that night mumbling his oft repeated invocation: "'To see the wave—its crest and foam....'" Liam looked up and smiled, but did not yet break the companionable silence.

By far, it was Tom's favorite room in the house, and Father Liam eagerly shared his hearth and library. The two young men felt as if they had known each other much longer than the few months of their acquaintanceship. Seemingly anxious for a responsive companion, Father Liam encouraged what must have seemed Tom's unending questions about the books they both devoured at every chance. They formed an immediate connection in their undisguised love for Jane Austen's small canon and often resorted to spontaneous in-depth analyses of particular characters and scenes only truly devoted fans can endure. Extra-textual conjectures relative to Anne Wentworth's well-deserved happiness and Mary Anne Brandon's possible regrets entertained them for hours. Some evenings they read silently together to the cadence of the locusts' song outside the open windows. Other nights they discussed any number of far-ranging topics as if familiar friends met after a long absence. Tom was totally at ease with Liam, who seemed to Tom to be much wiser and older, although actually Liam wasn't more than five years Tom's senior.

For Tom it was one of the most delightful times in his existence. As a relatively young man, to be taken seriously and treated with the utmost respect by such a universally esteemed figure as Father Liam made Tom immensely happy.

As if Tom were an expert instead of fresh out of college, Liam hounded Tom with questions about the latest theories of educational administration as he pounded out the details of the new school St. Patrick's was building. This was the project for which he had been assigned to St. Pat's by Bishop Guerke. Galveston was to have a Catholic school to rival the old, established private institutions in the East. The bishop had been explicit on only one point in his vague mandate: expense was of little consideration so long as the end result was a gem among stones. The bishop wanted the children of Texas's wealthy Catholics to send their heirs and inheritances to Galveston instead of Boston and New York and Philadelphia.

The perfect man for the job, Father Liam was tenacious in his quest to create the finest educational facility in his power. And Tom just as enthusiastically contributed any pertinent information from his studies to this real-life project while pelting Liam with questions of his own about everything from the personal histories of the children at the orphanage to the financial management of the large parish. In this de facto internship, Tom came to understand Liam still had few intellectual peers in Galveston and relished having another like-minded soul for companionship. The two were fast friends from their initial meeting.

"Liam," Tom said the evening of Lottie's party, ignoring the book in his lap. "Do you think anything is truly random? Serendipitous? Accidental? Does God allow instances in life to just happen? Like you coming to Galveston to build this school? Or me finding myself here doing whatever it is I'm supposed to be doing?"

"Well, that's a rather deep starter, Tom," Liam laughed, setting down his glass on the small table. "I'd hoped we might begin with how excellent Mrs. Tate's chowder tasted at dinner, but as you like. Being the incredibly certain man of faith that I am, I suppose the appropriate answer is, of course not. God knows everything; He plans everything; and knows exactly what will happen at all times to all people. Is it 1 John or 2 John? I can never recall—'God is greater than our heart, and knoweth all things.' So no, there is no randomness."

"Good. I like that idea," Tom responded lazily recollecting how nice the soup *had* tasted. He mused inwardly how philosophy seemed much more pertinent on a full stomach in the midst of a room such as this. "It's very comforting to know He's in charge somehow. That means I don't have to be. I suppose that's why I enjoy this line of thinking so much."

"Of course," Liam continued slowly and yet engaging in this insignificant ramble as eagerly as he studied the new building plans for the school structures. "Critics would suggest that line of thought leaves no room for free will. Our own choice. How can God know exactly what will happen if we truly have a will of our own and can change our minds at any time? That sort of thing." Liam surrendered his unread volume to the table between them.

"True," Tom volleyed, "but I don't see those two ideologies as mutually exclusive. God is God; He can and does know what will happen and what should happen if we do what's best for us or even if we use our free will and do something that isn't best for us. He knows which way we'll choose anyway, so doesn't that argue for the idea that there is no random element to our lives? We are here—wherever 'here' happens to be—because He guides our steps even if we think we decide on our own. Just because He's faster at knowing than we are when we make a split-second decision to change doesn't mean He didn't already know we were going to do that anyway."

"Yes," Liam agreed, "that's the mindset I ascribe to. We aren't able to *trick* Him by sleight of hand; He's the ultimate omniscient narrator, wouldn't you say? My dear father, who had a simpler but much stronger daily faith than I can claim, teased me as a child," he laughed fondly. "He was always assuring me on our walks that I might *just* be able to spin fast enough to see the hand of God changing my future if I tried hard. I smile now at our little game, but don't you think we do try to *catch* Him? I'm sure God does know what choices we're going to make even before we make them, which is much more than we know even about the simplest of decisions, so at least for God, there is no sense of *random*, if by that you mean something that has no set purpose. I know in my heart, everything has a purpose. It may just not be *our* purpose. That's where I fight God in my stubborn determination to do things my way."

Tom sat up farther in his chair as if to reach physically for this nagging idea just out of his grasp and continued, "So, if we suppose that God has placed everything in motion for a reason, which I do believe as well, how can you know with any degree of comforting certitude whether a choice you make is what God wants for you—since He knows all our choices anyway, and we can't surprise Him? I'm sure I increase my own problems greatly by assuming God is far too busy to attend to my miniscule affairs. You know, He has wars and famines to consider, so I won't bother Him. I used to ask for His help for really significant problems, but all else I would *handle* myself." Tom was speaking more to himself at this point, but Liam seemed in no rush to break the reverie so Tom went on.

"I mean no slight to what God is certainly capable of achieving. But I know I still do that sometimes. I try not to, but I simply see my little troubles as something I'd rather not burden Him with. Does that make sense? I realize too that I doubt my right to seek Him. I still wonder, Liam. Is our choice *God's* plan or simply that we *want* it to be God's choice, so instead of listening, we convince ourselves we're correct through dint of obsessive repetition and dogged stubbornness?" Tom sat back in my chair feeling tired all of a sudden. Too many questions. Again.

"I don't think we can know, Tom. We can try to figure it out and be as openly honest with ourselves as possible, and we can pray, of course, and discuss it with friends," Liam smiled at Tom as he said this, "but as for certitude? Absolute resolution? I'm not sure we get that."

"I just can't quite rationalize why I ended up here in Galveston, and by now I'm creeping into a nebulous time when even the rectory's generosity and hospitality will wear thin with my indecision. But where do I go? I have no desire to move to another parish or even to go back to my uncle and tell him I'm ready to give my life to the Church. That's my mother's fervent prayer, I know. *She* thinks that's what God wants— adamantly. I don't know what to do anymore." Tom sighed audibly.

Liam asked gently, "You're very confused about your vocation, aren't you? Is that what all this introspection is about?"

"I suppose," Tom conceded. "I know my faith is strong, but it's only my faith in God I'm sure about. I don't have such an overwhelming sense of connection to our Church or any church really to be able to say I know this is right. Right for me, anyway. I don't hate the Catholic Church at all; I'm sure of that. I don't know. Maybe it's all the rules. I study; I read; I pray…and I end up with more questions, not more answers. As if I *must* know for certain my life's path at once. Do you think God really wants us to think about Him as some sort of cruel dictator?"

"No, I'm fairly certain He hopes we'll study His word and then come to the right conclusions about love. Surely God hopes we obey the man-made rules you mention out of respect for Him and what He's done for us rather than from fear or some sort of rote obligation," Liam preached without condemning.

"Exactly," Tom agreed. "See? You and Uncle Tim have always understood the way I feel, but I don't think most people really believe that. Maybe I just haven't talked to very many people about this."

"I don't know about that, but I know many people do seem to see their journey as one of demands and regulations, as you mentioned. Life can be hard for people, but most difficulty, I think, people bring on themselves. My favorite lines from Milton—and honestly, I don't have too many—are how we make our own heaven and hell. I think Hamlet says the same thing, but I'm lousy at remembering exact quotes." He stopped and smiled at Tom before going on. "What brought all this to your mind? You certainly don't live your life slogging along as if in misery. As far as I can tell, you follow the rules *and* have a strong faith in God's mystery, don't you?" Liam asked kindly.

"I do. But it just seems…I just seem out of the norm in the way I perceive what church should be or at least *could* be," Tom started. "I never see anyone smile during Mass. I hear about the wonders Christ taught his followers in the familiar readings I love so much from my own study, and I look up and everyone around me is staring off stone-faced as if they don't realize what joy Jesus bought for us. I started noticing it a long time ago and mentioned it once to my mother, but she told me not to be difficult! That was pretty much the extent of the philosophical discussion in my home."

Liam laughed, "Well, that's one way to deal with our spiritual crises! Aren't mothers wonderful? Almost like a cure for indigestion. 'Just ignore those questions, Tommy; they'll go away!'" The friends both laughed a bit ruefully.

"I sense the goodness and joy God wants us to have, and I understand the need for discipline and respect, but I feel so weighed down by all the…what? What is that? The tension, I guess. Fear, maybe? A sense that if you step out of line, God's just waiting to strike you down—or He keeps some sort of long list of all our infractions and will throw it in our faces one day and demand retribution. I don't think God wants that for us. I see love in families and even just between friends outside of church, but it's as if too many people equate reverence with anger or at least a profound sadness so they can't be happy in church. No smiling! And absolutely no laughter! Joyful verses only for weddings and baptisms! But I don't seem to have too many supporters in that confusion beyond you and Uncle Tim."

"Maybe it's because we study the joy," Liam said slowly, smiling. "Most of our devoted flock own one huge and sanctimonious Bible kept high out of reach in a secure place of honor to ensure it is never opened, but cherished to record family milestones. If they are consistent, they will hear the entire Bible revealed to them once every three years. Thinking beyond that is painful for many or wearisome. That passivity is sufficient for them."

"Maybe. I don't know," Tom began again, "it's just that when I meet someone who gives cheerfully and is joyful and gets this idea I'm talking about, I realize that's exactly what God wants for all of us. And more often than that, I don't meet those few people at church. It's somewhere else. But maybe I'm wrong; I don't know."

Pausing slightly, Liam said, "I don't know either, my friend. Maybe we're not supposed to know. But, she *is* incredible, isn't she?"

"What? What are you talking about?" Tom snapped out of his reverie.

"Lottie," Liam said simply, "Lottie is incredible. I've never known anyone quite like her, and for one so young to be so in tune with everything going on around her—she's amazing. I thought you might agree."

"Well...I...I do," Tom stuttered feeling stupid in his sudden inability to utter simple words. "But...but how did you know I was thinking of Lottie just now? I thought we were discussing philosophical uncertainties. I've never mentioned Lottie to you that I recall."

"You haven't," Liam smiled at Tom. "Not directly at least. Have no fear that you've exposed her to unkind censure of any kind. You haven't, but I don't seriously believe I could think poorly of her in any case actually. I daresay no one else has noticed your regard. I simply supposed you were amazed by her in your few exchanges with her. Who wouldn't be? She has no equal hereabouts certainly."

"I am," Tom said slowly. "I am amazed. I didn't know I was, but I...I can't stop thinking about how amazed I am. I met her that day with William DeHaven, and she was immediately concerned about him. It was absolutely…sincere. I've never seen anything so…authentic, so nurturing. She was…amazing."

"And then our discussions today about educational reforms," Tom rushed on now, "She's obviously very intelligent. I doubt my sisters even know what *reform* means." Tom paused only for a moment. "You're right; I *am* amazed. But it's wrong. I shouldn't be saying this; I shouldn't even be telling you." Tom blurted these last words in a rush contradicting his very words in his relief to be able to speak finally of this all-consuming topic. Simultaneously, he was embarrassed to have articulated an idea that heretofore had been only a timid thought flitting on the edges of consciousness. Moments ago, it had been far less substantial. Now spoken, the germ was glaringly more real than any other thoughts vying for his immediate attention.

"Wrong?" Liam asked, sounding genuinely concerned. "Why is it wrong to notice how incredible another one of God's creations is, Tom?"

"For me, Liam," Tom explained quietly as if only now seeing the magnitude of these thoughts. "It's wrong for me. It's all true, but you know I'm not supposed to think about…things like this…like Lottie—or any other woman. Listen to me! Calling her

Lottie as if I had any right to such an intimacy! I astound myself. Not that any other woman could ever be like Lottie. Forgive me, Liam; I'm ranting. It's just.... Maybe that's why it was easier not to notice anyone this way before. It isn't as if I even know how to think like this. I've never consciously had to *not* think about being attracted to a woman. I guess I'm sad about having to stop thinking about who she is when I don't even understand her nearly well enough yet."

Liam spoke quietly now as well, "Well, certainly, you don't have to stop meeting her as you go about your days here. For one thing, she's determined, with my blessing, to play a significant role in the plans for the new school. And I depend on both of you to share your expertise."

"Lottie is more connected to children and how they think than most professional educators I've ever met," Father Liam continued. "She certainly reads up on the most current theories and the new developments the best schools in the East are implementing, but it's her natural connection with the children that interests me most. She knows what they need—what they *must* have in order to grasp concepts and behaviors we want to teach them. It's as if she has a special insight into the minds of people in general but especially with young children. And most impressively, it's all so natural and genuine. You've seen how they act around her; they truly love her."

He, too, was musing and far away as he contemplated this image of Lottie's redeeming qualities that had so quickly, and to Tom, so mysteriously, become the center of their discussion. Abstracting on the subject of Lottie Gallagher was becoming habitual to Tom, but he'd never discussed it openly. Liam broke the silence asking: "You've certainly thought about this, haven't you? Do you think you're in love with her, Tom?"

Tom looked up quickly to read his friend's face and sighed when he saw his eyes and understood Liam wasn't criticizing, just asking. "I have no idea. That can't be possible, can it? *Love* sounds so ominous. We've only just met; I don't even know her. But then other times, when we're talking or laughing together, I feel like I've known her for…well, for much longer. All of this sounds so banal out loud. In my mind, it's not…it's beautiful. I think about something she said and then all of a sudden I've been replying the whole scene over and over. And once I start, I can't seem to make myself stop thinking of her. If I *could* love someone, she's the only image I would want in that place."

Tom's words were coming out faster now as if he were trying to regain his balance. "She's first in my prayers and always in my dreams at night. I don't know what to do, Liam. And we were just saying God knew *this* would happen? Nothing up to this point in my life prepared me for this upheaval. I'm not supposed to feel this way. I've never been like this before." Tom stood up abruptly, throwing his unread book to the floor.

"It's perfectly normal, Tom," Liam said, speaking much more calmly than Tom was. "You've never felt this way, perhaps, because you've never permitted yourself to feel this way. You've mentioned a rather narrow focus to your upbringing all aiming at one end. Perhaps that isn't your end after all. Have you ever seriously thought of that? Did your parents allow you no other aspirations?"

"I don't know if *allow* is the right word exactly," Tom answered, trying to recall the details of a fuzzy image. His mind floated to the dormant lists—all dangling unresolved through his childhood—none offering up the answers he sought so dutifully. "I never remember even thinking of anything else, but I didn't feel coerced into something I didn't want. I just didn't ask for it, that's all. As if my future were our crowded dinner table, and I received a helping of Brussels sprouts. I never asked for them, but I ate them because they were there and offered. We none of us were asked our opinion or given choices. We merely accepted everything, I guess. Is that a terrible admission?"

"Well, it isn't necessarily terrible," Liam said, "although I'm not sure I would compare taking holy orders with odiferous vegetables in front of too many others if I were you—they may misunderstand." Liam smiled again in a concerted effort to keep the mood light. He continued, "Now back to you being in love with our Lottie. I'm trying to decide if I approve. You were saying?"

Tom surprised himself making a noise that sounded more like a groan than the sigh he had expected as he said, "Oh, Liam, don't joke. I don't know. How I despise not knowing! I thought I knew what God wanted me to do. I'm supposed to be the structured one, the calm one, the one who has it all in check and is proofed against all wavering. I have lists, you know!" Tom finally smiled, continuing, "I've always known what I was supposed to do to fulfill my part. I so desperately want to understand God's plan for me so I can serve Him with my whole being. Then I wonder how loving Lottie could possibly stop me from that purpose. Couldn't I do both? We could serve together. But I keep babbling, 'I don't know, I don't know' until I fear I'll go insane! I don't want to become some sort of cliché of a weak priest who uses the excuse of a woman just to avoid the rigors of the priesthood. I'm not afraid of commitment and sacrifice. I'm not. I do feel God wants me to serve Him. I just don't know how."

Tom didn't hesitate as he kept up his explanation speaking quickly now, "I always wanted everything to be just so. I thought if I had it totally organized then *I* would be in control. I made these idiotic lists that mean nothing ultimately. Once when I was very young, I made small paper cards very carefully with all my future plans on them. I think it likely that's where my current lists originated. I wrote out my next moves for my studies, my reading selections, my travel destinations—everything was very tidy. I would stack the cards a different way sometimes, but I was in charge of how they aligned themselves. It was so logical to have a plan and move forward with that plan. It was all ridiculously time consuming, of course; I certainly could have used my time more wisely, but it was orderly and distracted me from actually thinking, I suppose, and I took away a great deal of peace from that exercise. I've always thought my overwhelming sense of structure was my vocation. Now though! I don't know how to put away these thoughts I've never had before now that they're here. I don't want to slight God and the work I should be preparing to take on. Why do you think God brought me here if only to make me turn away from her?"

"Tom," Liam responded. "Tom, I'm sorry to have made light of your situation. You've obviously thought more about this than I had anticipated. I'm not laughing at you—it's more that I'm amused at myself and all of us really." He frowned, "I suppose *amused* isn't the right word, is it? We place such rules on ourselves for no apparent reason other than to have rules. First off, God *does* know why He brought you here even if we can't quite figure it out. We have plenty of evidence for that fact. We can only pray and know that all He does is for our good. I do know that much for sure. Give off worrying about that aspect and stand firm in your faith and conviction of this absolute truth."

"Next," Liam continued, "you *aren't* a priest, Tom. You are under no sort of pre-ordination obligation to forbid any type of secular relationship so long as you are chaste and honor God in that connection. And in saying that, I *am* speaking as your priest." He smiled at Tom to gauge his reaction.

Tom tried to smile back and whispered, "I know that, but this is so overpowering. Almost frightening in its intensity. I've never even imagined myself in this situation. It isn't as if I haven't been around women or couples before in my life, but I've never once thought that being with a woman is what I want or need as a part of my life. I am supposed to become a priest; my entire upbringing was directed toward that goal. And right now, I'm supposed to be deciding when to go start that process, but I've been wandering. I suppose I should be ashamed of my weakness, but I can never quite correlate the idea of shame and Lottie in the same thought. I want nothing but the very best for her and my thoughts of her are pure, I swear to you. It's just…they do exist."

"Even before I came here; even before I met Lottie, I've allowed the questions in my mind about being a priest to take shape that I'd always kept at bay as illogical and immaterial. My mother would never entertain any alternatives, but I kept wondering. I ask myself what else I could do or how I could still stay in God's favor and not be a priest after all this time. Now, I question if I've just been looking for some sort of excuse. Is that wrong? Is it wrong of me to think Lottie is an excuse?"

"Lottie may be *many* things to you," Liam smiled at Tom's still rambling, rapid-fire self examination, "but a bad excuse for being everything you have the potential to become? I doubt that. And God will not be disappointed with you or ashamed of you, Tom, if you remain a faithful servant to Him in whatever guise you choose. He surely does not what us to be simpletons who never argue or even question—why bless us with minds if He merely wanted constant submission and compliance?"

Liam smiled as he closed his eyes and said, "I was going to get married once. To Cassandra Victoria Elerby."

"Really?" Tom looked up surprised.

"Well, *I* thought I was," Liam smiled.

Tom replied, "I can't see that at all. You seem born to this life."

"Evidently, Cassie couldn't see it either," Liam continued, laughing. "I was devastated. How long ago that all seems now! She laughed at first and then cried when she saw I was serious. I certainly didn't run to the priesthood because I was rejected by Miss Elerby, but I wasn't born with this collar on, you know."

Liam became serious again, "The priesthood may still be your destiny, Tom, but taking orders is not the only sacramental vocation. Neither of the choices we seem to be considering are steps you should take lightly without due reflection and prayerful consideration. Perhaps Archbishop O'Rourke is even wiser than he appears to be on the surface. Marriage is a beautiful declaration of your promise to honor God through and with the help of another person." Liam stopped and smiled, "But perhaps now I *am* jumping to conclusions from Lottie being incredible, which I can second as a supportable truth, to her becoming your sacred helpmate! You have a lot of praying to do, but it doesn't need to take the tone of do or die. Try not to be anxious as you explore this angle. Does she know how you feel?"

"Heavens no, Liam," Tom answered too quickly, face reddening despite the cool breeze fluttering through the open windows. Tom continued to pace. "I've never even spoken the words out loud to myself until you coerced me into speaking. I asked about random actions and even then I believe I was half asleep. How did we get so far afield?"

"Lucky guess," Liam answered smiling.

"I don't think I could tell her, Liam. You seem so utterly calm about the whole thing! Doesn't this shock you? I'm not supposed to get married; I never was. I should just leave, shouldn't I? She could never love me anyway, and I'm sure her father wants much more for her. I have no prospects, no money to speak of, just me. That's not enough. I think I probably have to leave." Tom paused, turning to tread his well-travelled track, "Sooner rather than later, I think."

Liam spoke firmly but with a calm friendly tone, "Tom. Sit down. You aren't leaving tonight anyway. And I'm only calm because you're nervous enough for both of us. You may think you are, but you certainly aren't the first man to wake up one day and find out your life has turned upside down. We don't write our own scripts you know. I'm honored you shared all this with me. I think you have at least two issues here, my friend. And you owe it to yourself—and to Lottie—to think about both your potential vocations and to pray. Without guilt or anxiety or any sort of arbitrary deadline. I have an incredible trust that God will let you know which way is best."

He paused only slightly before adding, "Don't let anyone convince you that you are doing something wrong if you decide not to become a priest, Tom. Or if you do. Not your mother or anyone else. That's between you and God. Period. Whatever you do, you must be totally dedicated to God and live in the way He wants you to. This life certainly is only our stepping stone to eternal rest and reward, but God doesn't ask us to throw it away. You must not settle—not for any reason. God deserves better from us than that. I'm very content with my life as a priest because this is who I am; God has been so good to me, but I know men who are miserable and allowed guilt or pride or a stronger ego to direct their steps when only sincere communion with God should have been the guiding force. What a terrible waste and certainly not what He wants for us. Live the life God created for you."

"Thank you for your sincerity," Tom said, realizing Liam was the first true friend he had ever had. The sensation was strange but not unwelcomed; he felt physically lighter. "I've begun to think very few people in my life have been completely honest with me as if I wouldn't be able to cope with the truth. I only want to understand what God wants me to do."

9.   Summer Days

Jesus said, "Allow the little children, and don't forbid them to come to me; for the Kingdom of Heaven belongs to ones like these." Matthew 19:4

It was a perfect day for a picnic on the beach. The August heat made the prospect of wading in the surf irresistible. The children all wore similar suits of a nondescript blandness, sewn by the sisters who knew the simple practicality that children near the beach rarely remain dry, and the salt water would damage less serviceable garments.

Tom discovered later Lottie had conspired with Sister Bernadette, the swiftest and most able seamstress of the nuns, by ordering and donating this plain but comfortable material for the children's beach wear. She often took on tasks behind the scenes to help the sisters who would have lavished more time and attention on their beloved charges had money and tradition not stood firmly in the way. Lottie tried not to draw attention to her many gifts lest naysayers including Father O'Mallary deem her endeavors inappropriate or wasted.

Today's picnic was a celebration Lottie convinced the sisters they could pull off with so little complaint they should risk the censure. Lottie had wanted to have a singing picnic for the feast of St.

Cecilia, patron saint of music, but had no patience to wait for the actual feast day in November. A wee bit early for a hundreds year old saint surely wouldn't be criticized, would it? The sisters combined the day with a nature expedition to catalog the various shelled animals on the shore in science class for good measure, and the children delighted in the holiday feel of the day.

Lottie had brought cookies and fruits while the nuns organized games on the stretch of beach within walking distance of St. Mary's.

Father Liam and Tom arrived just as Mrs. Laraby, Lottie, Sister Bernadette, and the Mother Superior were helping the smallest children remove their shoes to play in the sand and surf.

"Stand still, darling," Lottie's smile belied the scold to her tiny charge. "How can I possibly get your shoes untied if you wiggle so much, Little One?!"

"Oh, but dear Miss Lottie," the child lisped and clapped her hands. "I'm so very gay; I could run on the sand forever!" She impetuously threw her chubby arms around Lottie's neck in her ecstasy.

Lottie laughed and hugged the girl back, saying, "Now you're free. Run and catch the gulls, Marie." Lottie lovingly watched the child run after the others.

"My dear father said those very words to me when I was just her size in France, Charlotte," Mother

Superior smiled at Lottie with a far-off look on her face. "What a lovely memory you have evoked, Dear."

Father Liam squeezed the older nun's proffered hand as he slightly bowed over it in a ritualistic gesture nonetheless respectful for its ancient origins. "I never knew you were from France, Sister," Father Liam said as he cordially greeted the others in turn with less ceremony.

"I never knew your name was Marie," Lottie added, smiling at the thought of her dear older friend scampering on a foreign shoreline as a child.

Sister Bernadette couldn't have realized how incredulous her stare was as Mother Superior smiled at her and said, "And I suppose, Sister Bernadette, you never knew I was a child?" The older woman's staid expression made it difficult to read as we collectively held our breath.

"Oh, no, Mother," Bernadette snapped out of her fixed look appalled at her lapse. "I never meant...I'm so sorry...I...please forgive me, Mother." She looked on the verge of tears, unsure if she should stop talking or continue to apologize.

The twinkle in her eye was the first hint of Mother Superior's good mood that day. We all exhaled as she said, "My sweet child, do not fret so! I believe what I said is commonly referred to as a jest. I was teasing you, Dear."

Sister Bernadette blushed to her roots and continued to stammer half apologies.

The whole group laughed when Mother Superior did, and she finally said, "Sister Bernadette, *you* forgive me, please. That I should have to explain small witticisms indicates I must be woefully out of practice! We'll begin anew by playing more. Gentlemen, you'll excuse us please if we play with the children. Sister Bernadette, would you be so kind as to help me remove my shoes?"

Ignoring the audible gasps of several nearby sisters, Mother Superior removed her high boots and stockings just as the children had. Smiling conspiratorially, Tom, Liam, and Lottie followed her lead, and soon were walking with bared feet and legs in the hot, murky brown water of the Gulf.

Tom said little that day, but watched everything. Mostly he watched Lottie, but she was involved in everything, he reasoned to himself later, so he was justified. The water wasn't cool, but it was wet and felt like summer.

One of the older nuns looked on the antics with barely disguised disapproval. She ventured a gentle remonstrance with her spiritual leaders.

"Mother Superior, I'm sure Father O'Mallary would question the appropriateness of our exposing the children to...." She left her image suspended.

"Sister Eugenia," Mother turned to her long-time work companion with a patience ingrained in her very nature. "I am sure the children will not suffer any long-lasting ill effects to learn their teachers and guardians are actually humans." She smiled gently but firmly refused to be censured. "And Father Liam is certainly official in his priestly role to guide us. In fact, I insist you join us, Sister. It will do you a world of good."

Liam smiled mischievously at the nuns' banter, "Fear not, Sister Eugenia, Jesus likely went barefoot on the beach as well, although I'd have to search for an actual biblical reference."

Tom was concerned Liam's jest was falling on deaf and disturbed ears until the two elderly nuns smiled at each other and actually giggled. Sister Eugenia looked 20 years younger instantly. Father Liam was a perennial favorite.

10. Revealed

The secret things belong to the Lord our God, but the things revealed belong to us and to our children forever, that we may follow all the words of this law. Deuteronomy 29:28-29

Time seemed to move at a ridiculously slow pace during this period, but in accordance with the great wisdom passed down through the ages, life certainly did move on despite Tom's tumultuous mind. Not too long after his heart-revealing evening with Liam, perhaps a few weeks, Tom's opportunity to do more than pray about Lottie came upon him without his realizing it was so close all along.

Just as the outward leg of an unknown journey seems so arduous in its tenuous twists and turns, this brief chapter of Tom's new life was a daily—sometimes hourly—debate on how to square his previous expectations with his present desires. The path is not so familiar and comforting; the missing puzzle section would so soon reveal itself as one at hand all along, only skewed from its present angle. Tom vacillated between practicing bold declarations in ridiculous coincidental meetings he imagined and doubt-filled escapes into a bleak, indefinable wilderness if he were now forced to live away from Lottie.

He wanted so desperately to declare his fervent regard for her, but worried how she might react to such rash behavior. Tom was scared. His mind reeled with thoughts of failure. Not just losing her esteem when he spoke any words of audacious amorous regard, but also knowing that once he spoke those words, they could never go back to what innocence they shared at this moment. There could be no more easy banter, no laughing interludes of friendship and mutual respect. Being unsure of her feelings toward him was not pleasant, but risking even the tenuous connection they now shared was debilitating. Tom was terrified at how real these ideas now were once spoken. He knew, if nothing else, he could never hope to subdue these ideas and images of a life with Lottie now, so if he were rejected, he would be forced to leave and remove himself from her home.

The thoughts Tom had fueled by speaking the ideas aloud to himself and to Liam seemed tangible, floating around him as he walked, bumping into him from behind when he wasn't paying attention, knocking him over out of the blue sometimes. The only power he held over them at this point was that he personally had not uttered these words to Lottie. The way she sometimes looked at Tom though made him wonder if his face and eyes were in league against him and had betrayed him to reveal how she possessed his heart and mind.

It didn't seem like such a different day when Tom had agreed to help the altar guild society sort the piles of donated clothes for the church bazaar one morning. They had been sitting for months in untidy piles in the large storage area at the back of the church. When first he had found the piles, Tom assumed they were rags for cleaning. He was kindly but firmly instructed to be ready by nine, to begin sorting the clothes into sizes. Tom wasn't particularly drawn to this type of task, but his only job at the church was to find work needing to be done. The older ladies were kind to Tom, bringing him food maternally, but they often fell into an innocent enough banter while they worked, not quite gossiping, but projecting their random thoughts on how one or another of the parishioners would turn out. It made Tom tired, but they seemed renewed by the speculation. They married people, buried others, lost some totally irascible types at sea, and produced numerous babies over stitching tables and tall sweating glasses of watery tea.

The slow pace of everything on the island, due no doubt to the oppressive heat almost all year was still not something Tom could easily adjust to. Galveston had no seasons! How could anyone mark the passage of time? Tom tried not to seem impatient as he sat with groups such as the altar guild contributing wherever he could to the endless tasks involved in the running of the parish, still wondering about his place here.

Tom much preferred other jobs, even the manual labor of maintaining the large structure and grounds. He thoroughly enjoyed time at the orphanage and visiting the people too old or sick to come to Mass, but he reminded himself often that it wasn't his place to decide in what ways he was supposed to serve. Tom wasn't here to enjoy himself; he was here to…what?

What was he here for? He knew he was lingering. How much of that was about Lottie? He had never stayed this long in any one place on his journey to discover his mission as Uncle Tim had called it when they had spoken privately after Tim's momentous announcement to Tom's parents. One part of Tom's brain hurried to brush away any serious contemplation about his current location. Another part of his brain stayed there constantly.

"Mr. McDermott," the perky committee chairman hailed from the gateway into the churchyard where Tom was pulling a few missed weeds. "You have made this yard look so lovely again. I simply adore what you have done." Mrs. Eleanor Laraby, a very pretty, very tiny woman of no discernible age, was originally from Mobile, Alabama, and she simply adored a great many things, Tom had noted since he came to

Galveston. He smiled and waved as she bustled up the walk. She didn't seem like much of a worker, impeccably dressed as always in outfits that somehow seemed a bit nicer than her neighbors could muster. But she donated large sums of her husband's cotton money to parish projects, volunteered countless hours tending the rose gardens around the church building or sending her servants to do so, which was the same thing in her mind, and was always cheerful. For all of those reasons, Tom was grateful for her. He often escaped behind her convivial chatter since she didn't seem to mind or even notice if she were the only one talking in a conversation. Tom liked Mrs. Laraby.

Mrs. Laraby was a flutterer and rarely stayed on task long. She had fully intended to assemble a large group of idle neighboring women to sort the faded castoffs for the church donation tables, but she walked toward Tom with only one other. He knew instantly it was Lottie, and he hoped he didn't blush in his happiness to see her. Tom immediately chastised himself to control his emotions around her. Even if he were able to hide it from everyone else, as Tom was certain he had, this was untenable ground to be on. Facing her in this manner, Tom could no longer deny he lingered at St. Patrick's more for the possibility of this type of chance meeting with her than any other reason he could conjure.

Just as Tom espied Lottie, Mrs. Laraby spoke again, "I'm just not certain if you two young people know each other or not, but Mr. McDermott, this is Miss Charlotte Gallagher, my dear, dear friend. She is an angel to me really. Charlotte, dear, this is Mr. Thomas McDermott; he's working here at St. Patrick's for the time being. And I'm sure we've never been so blessed."

Lottie blushed as she laughed, looking to Tom every bit as angelic as Mrs. Laraby had claimed. She directed her words at Mrs. Laraby but included Tom, "Eleanor, you exaggerate so! Of course Mr. McDermott and I know each other. We've met dozens of times. Don't you remember our picnic on the beach with the children just last week?"

"Lottie," Mrs. Laraby beamed, "of course, you're right, as usual. I do recall that now, but our darling Mr. McDermott is such a quiet soul. You were both so busy taking care of those poor, unfortunate children. I'm sure the sisters simply adore your help. And the older boys especially, Mr. McDermott, need to be in the company of good men such as yourself far more often. But, I declare I never once saw the two of you so much as exchange a word. Do let's change that today, shall we? Young people need to visit with others like themselves, my dears. You both do far too much for others without a word of complaint; today can be a fun change for you with no one else to bother us."

Tom wondered silently if Mrs. Laraby realized her irony as the group turned to their charitable task for the day. Of course, he said nothing.

As if she needed to explain some humor Tom may be missing in their exchange, Lottie smiled, "To translate that, I'm afraid the two of us are it, Mr. McDermott. Elly forgot to ask anyone else early enough, and everyone on our small committee must have much more fascinating daily lives than I do."

Tom smiled, inwardly praising God for giving him exactly what he'd hoped, and spoke instead to the two of them trying to maintain the levity Lottie had intended. He said, "Well, then, we'll just have to pray the others have arranged such noble ways to gain entrance to Heaven for themselves and forge ahead without them!"

The women laughed, and the trio began. Throughout the morning, they all continued their mindless task. Mrs. Laraby was right; Tom and Lottie were able to chat more easily than when prying ears were present, and they passed the time amiably. Tom was happy to be engaged so pleasantly even when they didn't talk. He enjoyed the simple company, but his mind was not needed in the chores of stacking and folding the small garments, so he could barely contain it from its now favorite pastime of devising comparisons to Lottie's beauty.

Knowing he could never love her and possess her in the way the lovers in his books expressed their passion didn't seem to alert Tom's mind to the futility of this activity. It was simply a way to lull himself to sleep on restless nights or while away a sleepy afternoon, he had convinced himself. It was simply another of Tom's lists. He often realized he was doing it only after he had been well into a mental search for any object or thought he could use to match her.

His catalog was probably typical. He'd seen the smooth marble faces of the Greek goddesses in the books Uncle Tim shared with his favorite nephew. Helen's face was indubitably the image men would conjure when off to war, but that wasn't quite the right connection. Lottie's delicate features were likely in the dreams of several wealthy local men, Tom thought with an inward frown. She was certainly beautiful in a regular sort of way, and he knew that's what the statues were supposed to represent, but they were coldly perfect in a way that somehow didn't resemble Lottie. Her blush was singular in its dusty pink shade just visible high on her cheeks, not a harsh red blotching her face. What would have been kindly corrected by the artist's brush only added to her beauty.

Her top lip that always seemed puckered up playfully; her left eye that drooped almost imperceptibly on her high cheek such that she often appeared to be looking down through her lashes. Her hair must curl naturally because no man-made contraption could make waves such as surrounded her small head in a glow of light reddish softness. Clouds during a particularly brilliant sunset came to Tom's mind with a seamless blend of soft pinks and bright oranges and dynamic yellows, but that comparison didn't seem quite accurate either. She always wore her hair up, so Tom could only wonder how long it was. He envisioned her hair streaming out behind her as she ran down the beach as a child and wondered how high it would lift with the sea breeze now, no longer a child in any way.

Tom must have spent the better part of the morning in such contemplations, hoping he hadn't stared at her throughout their work because he didn't realize it was noon until the downtown whistle blew its daily reminder for the dock workers. Evidently, Mrs. Laraby didn't notice or attend to Tom's lack of attention for his work. She had rambled gaily on talking about everything and nothing, he assumed. Tom only glanced up when some story elicited a laugh or comment from Lottie, who seemed as content as he was to allow Mrs. Laraby to regale them.

As the whistle brought them all back to the task at hand and the passage of time, Mrs. Laraby jumped up scattering the tiny baby sweaters she held in her lap. They had moved to the tables just outside the storage room in the church garden to have more room for the growing stacks of different clothes.

"Oh, dear me," Mrs. Laraby exclaimed in her perpetual excitement, "I had no idea it was so late. I promised my little Matthew I would be home to read him his naptime story and feed the bunnies their lunch! Where did the time go, you darling, darling little worker bees?" She began to gather her upset pile of clothes and prepared to leave the impromptu work area. "Let me just clean up this mess with you…."

Lottie spoke Tom's thoughts, which delighted him more than it should have, he knew even then. She said, "Elly, you go on to Mattie and give him my love and a kiss on his adorable nose. I'll help Mr. McDermott clean this up. We're so close to finishing you know. It will only take a few more minutes. We ended up being the most efficient committee I've been on in a very long time! Then I'll be along shortly to see you and Mattie; he is expecting me after his nap."

"Oh, Charlotte," Mrs. Laraby smiled at her young friend, "would you? You are such a darling to me. And my little Matthew, Mr. McDermott, he just dotes on our dear, sweet Charlotte. He cries himself to sleep when he can't see her. In fact, he's such a naughty rascal, the only punishment I can devise with any effect is to tell him he'll not be able to see his Miss Lottie if he's ill natured!" She laughed fondly at the memory of her child and smiled at Lottie with maternal gratitude.

"Now, Mrs. Laraby," Tom began teasing along with her, "that course of action seems a bit harsh. He is merely a child; how can you be so mean as to keep him from his playmate? I do hope you reserve that punishment for very serious infractions only."

Mrs. Laraby laughed but shook her head insisting, "It's the only thing that has any influence whatsoever, I swear."

"Both of you are so foolish," Lottie laughed blushing instantly as she began carrying stacks of clothing back into the organized categories she had prepared in the store room as if to remind Tom of his recent contemplation of the exquisite color of her blush. They all started walking toward the front side of the church building to see Mrs. Laraby to the front gate. As they saw her pass out of sight toward her nearby home, Tom felt the first drop of rain on his arm. He looked at Lottie, and she was already dashing for the door of the church they had just walked past. Tom rushed in behind her feeling a little breathless and lied to himself that the cause was the brisk run.

"We're not supposed to be here, are we?" Lottie cooed an easy laugh as she hurried out of the rain still holding the clothes she had been sorting when Mrs. Laraby realized she was late. She wasn't irritated by the sudden rain that assuredly would mar her garments or concerned with the mess the two would certainly face upon returning to their work. She was wholly immersed in the moment that struck her as a kind of pleasant adventure. Tom allowed himself to revel in the primitive emotional intensity of simply being near her. He wondered if he'd ever known anyone else who seemed so content. Tom knew being alone with her for the first time would impact him somehow; she was just so lovely, he wondered if anyone could ever get enough of her beauty to last a lifetime; to create the kind of mental pictures you couldn't erase no matter how far away you ran or what you tried to convince yourself was more important or more a part of your being than basking in her glow.

Not only had Tom never been alone with Lottie, he'd never been allowed by generations of repression to see her with wet hair straining at her attempts to confine it, never allowed to concentrate on the glorious flush the sudden exercise had created that started in her lovely cheeks and continued beyond her neckline where even his fervent imagination stopped before losing all sense of control and decorum. Forcing the heat in his own face to abate by sheer will, he thought of all the philosophy he and Liam had discussed regarding this very topic and realized suddenly they'd merely touched the trembling surface of all the conflicting thoughts and emotions Tom held inside about this woman.

Tom finally dared to speak, "No—here's fine, I think." He looked around the weekday quietness of the church he'd come to love so much in the past months. What was he thinking? His mind was racing with his earlier nonsensical comparisons—nothing ever would equal her, he knew abruptly.

"It's here I'm not sure about," Tom thought, touching his breast pocket and unwittingly catching Lottie's attention with the seriousness of his expression.

"I don't understand," Lottie frowned, "I can leave if you want me to."

"No. Please don't. It's all right," Tom rushed to retain her, sounding too urgent even to himself. "You said you don't understand. Neither do I, I guess." She relaxed and smiled, which was probably Tom's downfall or salvation, however history wants to write this story. He started again emboldened by her calm, "You may not like this, and I don't want to ruin some sort of spell we seem to have when we are together. I have been so very happy these past few weeks—months really." Tom knew he was talking too fast, but something from far away compelled him to take this one chance. He could be out of town in a few hours without a trace left behind for people to worry about—he'd done that before, but right now he had to tell her. This very minute.

"Miss Gallagher...no, Lottie. Lottie, I know I have no right to speak to you this way. To call you by your name. I know I'm not...I'm not supposed to feel this way. I just can't seem to help myself. Ever since I came here, I've been drawn to you for some reason I can't explain away. I tried to ignore it, but I admit I cannot. But I know I'm not supposed to think like that, and I know you can't feel this way, too." Tom wasn't sure how she looked when he said these words. He couldn't bear to see some scathing retort on her beautiful face, but he knew he had to force the words out or suffocate from them for the rest of his life. It all seemed to make so much sense to him on that day; it really didn't matter what she said or did after he told her, but Tom would have made sure she understood his heart.

When she spoke, her words didn't sound filled with disgust and anger; she whispered, with a tone Tom thought sounded like wonder, and said, "What way, Tom? I do think I know what you're saying, but....Did I do something wrong?" Despite the fact that Tom should have been wholly and exclusively focused on her exact words and the message she was conveying to him, totally concentrating on the gravity of the situation and what he was doing, he couldn't control his heart from being thrilled when she so comfortably and naturally dropped all pretense and called him by his given name, even his just-for-friends informal name, for the first time; it sounded so right in her voice. Tom's name had been on her lips—could he have done anything but delight in that? But he did note in his foolish abandon that she also sounded distressed, which spurred him to correct that error.

"Oh, no, you didn't do anything wrong." Tom assured her. You could never do anything wrong. It's me." Tom could tell his mind was flitting to the edges of what was now so clearly an insane passion for Lottie. It was all about to be over, he lamented inwardly. This lovely, soothing dream world. This nocturnal charm for warding off the most persistent sleeplessness. Tom never *did* anything with Lottie in his world; he was simply allowed to stay there with her; soon even that would be gone. Tom was a few insignificant steps from causing his own banishment from the only place he had ever wanted to belong; he was sure of it. She would likely be kind about it; Tom mused, which would only make it all the worse. He felt like an idiot.

How did this happen in novels? They could be Tom's only guide here; he had no idea what he was doing. He wanted to declare his love to her and learn his fate. Regardless of his doom, he longed to know what was in Lottie's mind. More than that, he wanted to propose to her on one knee that they stay together forever regardless of other obligations or commitments or the expectations of the rest of the world. But this wasn't the place; this wasn't the time. To know his heart would have to stay with her permanently regardless of what her reaction was to his confession. Perhaps he should stall a bit longer.

Every fiber of Tom's being strained to tell Lottie he loved her.

His mind ran wild with conjuncture: "What would she say to me? Me? I, of all people, Mr. Almost-a-Priest-but-Can't-Quite-Decide-McDermott!   To declare love to a beautiful woman! *This* beautiful woman! A woman who doesn't know me from Adam.

What in the world could the poor girl say to that? Honestly! Doubtless I was wrong to be so bold. I won't do it now," he resolved.

"I'll just have to live not knowing to spare her the certain embarrassment it would cause her to reject me. Ah, but to never know! She likely couldn't even fathom that I had such expectations of any return of my now undeclared devotion."

Tom had been ruminating so long an awkward tension pervaded the space between them. Tom was embarrassed by his unkindness to her.

Lottie's silence scared Tom or made him terribly nervous and even more reckless, he couldn't tell which. All his previous resolve, his heroic conviction to remain silent and live a hermit's life as the more noble act than to subject her to his maniacal ranting dissolved into oblivion in her inquisitive look and what Tom then took as her angelic patience. Against his characteristically logical nature and contrary to anything close to sane behavior, Tom continued in the same vein, only this time it was out loud, "I do regard you…most highly, I think. I guess. No, I know *that* if I know nothing else." He thought "Why was this so blasted difficult? I'm babbling."

"Just leave," Tom told himself and promptly ignored himself again, continuing aloud, "I…I certainly feel…strongly—very strongly—about you, Charlotte Gallagher. And I'm not supposed to." Tom feared he would start weeping or laughing hysterically.

By this point Tom truly seemed to be talking to someone else, or perhaps to no one in particular, just rambling as he continued rushing through thoughts that may have formed many, many years ago and only now he could formulate into coherent words. Regardless of their origin, he continued "Or maybe that's not quite right either. Maybe I *am* supposed to feel this way because—well, who could help it really? But…but, I'm not supposed to *tell* you or *do* anything about it because that's not what God wants for me? If that's true, then this is my sacrifice? Is that it?" Gesturing, he began to pace in the empty church as he went on. "Could God ask so much of one man?" Flashes from his unusual, lonely childhood danced feverishly through Tom's throbbing head as he knew he would have willingly given up far more than he did had loving Lottie ever been his life goal.

Lottie shifted her head just a fraction; not impatiently, simply listening. Her wet hair still strained for release, but the small movement was enough for the waft of warm fragrance to divert Tom's thoughts to her incredibly feminine beauty and away from the recitation of this infantile philosophy of destiny as she spoke in the softest of whispers but with a conviction Tom could not misinterpret, "Oh, Tom. I am so sorry. Truly I am. I...I thought it was just me, and it wouldn't matter that way. I never meant to get you in trouble. Saints above! You know as well as I do Father O'Mallary won't like this one bit, will he now? Why do I always seem to cause such problems for people I love so dearly?" She trailed off rubbing the side of her finger in a habit Tom had noticed before but had never seen as so enchanting.

Tom stared at her puzzled face. Could she actually have said what he thought she said? Running his words together, at least an octave higher than usual, Tom asked, "*Am* I one of those? You love me? Can that really be true, Lottie? Do you know what you said? Listen. You said: 'for people I love so dearly.' Could you actually love me? So dearly? Say it again."

Her troubled expression vanished into a warm smile as she ascertained, nodding, "Well, of course you are. Aye, I've always loved you, Tom. Even before you came, I think, but you wouldn't understand that part of it. I will tell you one day, though. I knew I loved you when first I saw you...but I knew you...couldn't love me because you belong to God, and I'm just me who doesn't, not in any special way that is. I supposed, silly girl that I am, that I could manage it if I could be close to you, and I was managing. Honestly. But, oh, why did I have to go and ruin everything?! Now we won't be able to meet and be ever the best of friends. I just hate that! I think we could have made do being friends, don't you?"

She ended as flushed with consternation, the beauty of which did nothing to remind Tom of his once-all-consuming religious vocation. Even her pout seemed cherubic to Tom, flushed as he was with the impossible declaring itself so loudly as truly and decidedly possible. His mind was reeling! He tried not to allow all his negative images of leaving and living alone to morph into instantaneous positive thoughts, but these attempts were feeble and ultimately futile. He asked himself, "*Could* we be together from this point on? Really together all the time? Could I actually...marry her? I've never even held her hand or kissed. Could we stay together forever?"

Taking up Tom's previous tone, Lottie continued in an animated voice, "Father O'Mallary lost no time in calling to tell me of my sinful ways! I must be fair and not exaggerate; he is a good man...deep down. He merely wanted to inform me what a promising future you had in the priesthood. That made entire sense to me, of course. You are obviously brilliant; Father Liam is impressed with you and your potential. And I can see that when we talk. I do so enjoy talking to you, Tom. I didn't mean to think about you as often as I did; it just seemed natural to wonder what you were thinking and doing—nothing out of the ordinary. I know I should have been more cautious when I did know what you were expected to become. I do *know* the rules, of course. I never intended to come between you and God's plan for you. I have no excuse; it's just that I've not ever met anyone like you, Thomas. You're just like me, and I've never known another person like us. Everything feels so right when you're with me."

Her eyes were so bright Tom could never have doubted her tenacity, but hardly dared to expect such sweet affirmations when his mind had long convinced his heart it was lost to a course that could promise only dismay and rejection. To hear this exquisite sound must be akin to aborigines first hearing a symphony. Not responding only to the composition of the actual music but becoming aware that sound so lovely exists! How can a feeble mind grasp that level of beauty?

Tom was stunned. Near speechless. He knew now he was staring because Lottie looked at him and smiled a crooked, worried smile as if she were a petulant child hoping a distraction would save her from punishment. Unable to quench his thirst, Tom continued to stare, so Lottie repeated herself without being asked.

"Of course I love you, Thomas. I thought I hid it from everyone. For just a little while I hid it even from myself. I didn't much like myself then, and I'm certain no one around me did! Then I just decided I would allow myself this one selfish luxury. I suppose that was wrong of me, wasn't it? I couldn't see how it would hurt anyone, least of all you. But now, this—this revelation does quite complicate things, doesn't it?"

She seemed so at ease with this world-upending confession as if somehow she had truly been anticipating Tom's coming, knowing he would love her. It wasn't arrogance; it was all-encompassing confidence as if she had planned this convergence long ago and watched with a satisfied air as the pieces fell together correctly. But how could she know that if Tom didn't? Tom felt like a fish gasping to return to water. He uttered, "I...I...what," but his tongue wouldn't cooperate in delivering what he hoped would pass for articulation. His joy at her words, his confusion at how to proceed—this definitely was not the outcome Tom had expected of this afternoon.

The rain was still washing the old away outside. But as the minutes continued to pass, despite Tom's world contorting from its long-held trajectory, he realized he definitely could see her in such a different light. Of course she loved him! He rejoiced to himself, "Of course! This is why God brought me here." To Lottie, he exclaimed, "Can you possibly know how blessed I feel right now? How could you know how I love you?"

Lottie's anxious flush melted into a lovely glow as she turned to him, "I have prayed for a long time for you to come to me, dear, dear Thomas. But what shall we do? What will Papa say? What will Father O'Mallary say? You're supposed to be determining your course, he says. You're to become a great priest someday, maybe a bishop or even a cardinal. That work doesn't include me." She looked away with a frown.

"At present," Tom started, realizing he needed to be careful how he worded these first acknowledgements even to himself, "you're right. I *did* come here to determine my course, and I thought I knew pretty well what that course was to be and how it looked and what I would do to serve God in thanksgiving for all my blessings, but…."

"But what, Mr. McDermott?" Father O'Mallary's harsh tone was unmistakable despite the noise from the rain on the roof, and neither of the lovers had heard him enter from the side vestibule. They both jumped as if guilty of some heinous crime.

"Father," Lottie began nervously, "I didn't hear you come in."

"Obviously. I think this would be a good time for you to go along home, Miss Gallagher," Father O'Mallary's tone had shifted to a malevolent glee that froze Tom's blood. He seemed to enjoy their discomposure. Tom checked the anger he felt rising. Anger that their beautiful moment had been so harshly interrupted. Anger that this man of God so delighted in what he saw as a compromising situation. Anger that anyone would dare think ill of Lottie in such a way. And anger that his own rash emotions had actually placed his beloved angel in such a seemingly negative light by his lack of self control. The rapidity of the diverse emotions coursing through him made Tom feel lightheaded and almost sick.

Tom turned to face the priest, "I'll take Lott— Miss Gallagher home, Father." Tom tried to control his breathing knowing he should not confront this man's anger at what he presumed had occurred. Tom thought, "What did he think had occurred? What had occurred?" His mind was empty, but he desperately ached to be alone with Lottie before he lost all sense of what had just passed and what lay ahead of him now.

"No, Mr. McDermott. I think not," the older man droned now, evidently taking a childish joy in being nominally in charge. "I could ring your father, my dear," Father O'Mallary directed his face toward Lottie.

"No, Father," she answered a bit too fast in her resignation Tom thought. Lottie spoke with her typical kindness and respect, but totally in control of herself as she bade the men farewell, "I believe the weather has cleared some; I'll be fine the few blocks to home. The fresh air will do wonders for me, I'm sure. Good day, Father. Mr. McDermott." She nodded at Tom slightly as she passed by with a regal movement.

Tom didn't have long to wait to hear how distorted the priest's version of their monumental but innocent encounter was. Father O'Mallary's outrage soared far beyond any rational explanation and regardless of what part of the conversation he had heard, he took on the role of warden for Tom's alleged transgression, which seemed to worsen with each passing hour after he ushered the young man out of the sanctity of the church he implied Tom had sullied by his wayward and sinful actions.

Father O'Mallary would hear nothing from Tom, rather he lectured him on his lack of ambition, his blinding confusion, and his obviously erroneous assumptions of his obligations at St. Patrick's as a guest. Rather quickly the words blurred and became an annoying buzz. None of his ranting and righteous indignation mattered to Tom; nothing mattered except her. Tom loved Lottie, and she loved him. Imagine that! How could anything in the world matter other than this simple, beautiful truth? It was all he knew and all he needed to know. Everything was perfectly clear now. All his wandering was at an end. Liam was right, of course. How could Tom have doubted it? He was *not* here by accident—God *did* have a purpose for him, and Tom had just seen that purpose in the trusting sage-colored eyes of his bride.

11.   Calm

They were glad when it grew calm, and he guided them to their desired haven. Psalms 107:29-31

Tom tried to sort out his racing thoughts as he sat in his room at the rectory a few hours later, only released from Father O'Mallary's wrath by the intervention of the weekly Parish Council meeting, grace for which Tom would be eternally grateful. Unfortunately, this administrative exercise also took away the succor he assuredly would have enjoyed had Tom been able to speak with Father Liam even if only for a few minutes. He would have understood.

But for now, Tom took solace in being alone away from the drone of Father O'Mallary's incessant litany of abuse. He so vehemently desired Tom's admission of guilt and some show of shame and contrition. He had no interest in divining the truth. Tom reasoned and understood the old man couldn't know the sequence of events had come to Tom as such a delightful surprise. That Father O'Mallary had no room in his old heart to allow for any other conclusion than the one he had jumped to when he saw Lottie and Tom together saddened Tom on a much grander scale than he expected. One blind and bitter man would not stop Tom from fulfilling his God-ordained future; but he also realized Father O'Mallary would never change.

He would continue to doubt and judge and condemn long after today. That wasn't right.

Pacing notwithstanding, Tom decided purposeful activity would serve him better than this languid wash of abstraction he was floating in. He left the rectory and headed toward St. Mary's. Tom only settled on this destination because the orphanage and school was far enough away to provide him with a mind-airing walk. Tom could imagine any number of paths to move toward after today's enlightening exchange with Lottie. None of these mental routings were clear as of yet, but he was sure his giddy state kept a great deal of reality out of the plans. What incredible power and peace he felt in this new-found knowledge! He repeatedly mumbled, "Amazing!" so many times he seemed daft even to himself.

"She loves me!" he mumbled walking thought the balmy afternoon. "This morning I was just me; now I'm…well, me, but so different! She actually thinks about me while we're not together. How incredible."

Tom immediately wanted somehow to be a better person so those precious thoughts of hers weren't wasted. Something she could be proud of—someone she wanted to introduce to others as hers.

Aware of everything and nothing simultaneously, Tom walked slowly and sprinted mentally. He wanted to scream out and tell strangers in the street how elated he was. He could barely stand having no fixed employment or even a permanent residence for that matter. He thought, "I need to settle now so we can begin our lives together."

Uncharacteristically for him, Tom harbored no doubts whatsoever that this jubilation may be one-sided; nor did he entertain any sense of caution that he should possibly temper his joyful anticipation lest he be disappointed when some altercation changed his current bliss. He was more certain of Lottie's love than he had been about anything in his life.

Without realizing he had traveled so far, Tom looked up to see the two familiar wooden dormitory buildings that comprised the majority of St. Mary's small grounds. The large simple structures predominated the landscape in this area. The sisters and their young charges were well liked and supported as neighbors. Many of the younger children were outside and several waved at Tom as he walked through the simple cross-shaped gate with the familiarity of an old friend.

William DeHaven was one of the older students assigned to oversee the children's playing. As he approached at a run, Tom saw William was holding a stiff card.

"Hi, Mr. Tom," William called smiling. "I was coming up to St. Pat's as soon as Sister Mary Ellen came back for the kids. I have a note from Cashlin for you."

"Cashlin?" Tom asked confused.

"Mr. Robert himself brought it to me. And was he ever hurrying. It must be pretty important cuz he was really serious and told me about 100 times to make sure you got this and that nobody else at church took it for you," William said as he handed Tom the note. "Tell Mr. Robert I did it good, will ya, Mr. Tom?"

"You did your task *well*, William. Thank you. I will tell Mr. Robert," Tom spoke automatically taking the offered sheet.

Tom's confusion changed instantly into awed admiration. The note's few words confirmed his intuitive assessment: Lottie *was* as excited as he was about their mutual recognition and admission of love and the ramifications of this newly formed venture, but she certainly was not as immobilized and befuddled as Tom seemed to be. She acted. Her beautiful handwritten note read:

Dear Friends,

Let us bid a fond farewell to summer with one more picnic at Cashlin tomorrow,

Saturday, September 8. Please plan to spend the afternoon with us from noon onward.

With kindest regards,

Charlotte Gallagher

In a smaller script at the bottom of the thick ivory parchment, in a slightly shaking hand, she wrote:

Tom—

> *This was the most expedient plan I could devise at a moment's notice. I long to meet with you again and continue our fascinating conversation from earlier today. My thoughts and prayers are with you as I wait eagerly to see you.*

L

Brilliant! As Tom read and reread her sweet yet conspiratorial message, he was thrilled with her socially acceptable plan and certainly her quick-witted strategy. They did need to talk, of course, and now they could. "Beautiful *and* intelligent! How could I merit all this?" Tom thought. He smiled so wide he felt his cheeks stretch over his teeth. Tom risked becoming idiotic again, so he propelled himself into action.

Tom held the precious card focusing on composing himself enough to endure not seeing Lottie for the ensuing hours of this night and tomorrow morning. No small task that. Buoyed with her confidence and devotion though, he made clear decisions. Borrowing materials from the sisters, he penned a quick reply to Lottie, strictly forcing himself to control any fervent expressions of his admiration but simply assuring her of his prompt attendance.

Tom also wrote briefly to Liam explaining the situation, again ordering himself to forego scripting a lengthy missive in defense of the spurious story Father O'Mallary certainly had plied Liam with at the Parish Council meeting. As a kindred spirit with Liam, Tom knew confidently, the two of them would have time soon for these long discussions. He secured Sister Mary Ellen's permission to have William deliver the messages. The young boy promised again to place these notes only in the hands of the recipients and seemed pleased to have been entrusted with them.

Then Tom arranged for temporary lodgings at a small hotel near St. Patrick's to remove his somewhat awkward presence at the rectory for the immediate future. He was loathe to seem to acknowledge any semblance of wrongdoing by fleeing, but also refused to subject himself to more of Father O'Mallary's closed-minded accusations and false judgments.

Now was a transition time. Tom realized he could not expect others to have the same comfort with this change of mind and stated life purpose immediately. His thoughts suddenly flashed to his mother's pained and anxious face as he had started on this journey away from her. He pushed the image aside. Change is difficult at any time, but change can be good. This change was essential. Tom vowed to himself that he would endeavor to show the others that truth, and they would then be able to share in his happiness.

That was the morning of Friday, September 7, 1900, the day Tom would forever note as the day life truly began. Even had the next day's events not forced its way into his consciousness and into the world's collective memory, he would never forget that day as long as he lived.

12.   Artie

Yet you do not know what your life will be like tomorrow. You are just a vapor that appears for a little while and then vanishes away. James 4:14

Glancing once more at her elegant handwriting on the invitation he had received an hour before, Artie sighed. He tossed the third identical white shirt to the bed where the intricate overstitching the tailor had painstakingly tightened on each cuff fell to the ornate rug as unceremoniously as an errant rag from the chambermaid's cache. Artemus Rutherford Hayes Morgan wasn't usually dismissive of the many lovely trappings wealth brought to his everyday movements. In fact the servants at Overton House preferred the young master to his gruff father.

Artie enjoyed interacting with the household staff; they were kind to the boy as he stumbled through his awkward youth with an overbearing father and vacuous mother. He was amiable, cooperative, and essentially listless, flitting from one interest to another, never quite able to set his mind long on any significant pursuit. Today, however, he was even more distracted than was his norm. He mumbled to his mirror, "Charlotte…I would esteem you…."

"Blast it," Artie blurted as he tugged the next starched sleeve over his puffy hand.

"Just say it out, you fool," Artie unwittingly mimicked his father's oft heard remonstrance to his downcast reflection.

"Yes," the image replied, emboldened by the taunt and encouraged by his constant pre-occupation with how he could secure the acceptance of Charlotte Gallagher if only he could form an articulate declaration. "I'll just say to her..." he began. "I'll go up to her...and I'll say, 'Charlotte, we have played together....' No, no, no, Idiot, that won't do. It's trite. Think!"

He often argued with himself this way—a habit his father despised. "Fine, I'll say, 'Charlotte'— everyone else calls her Lottie, you stupid bore. Right...right" He took a deep breath and began again. "I'll say, 'Lottie, it cannot have missed your observation....' Perfect, now you're openly claiming she's too dumb to see that you drool every time you're with her. Try again."

Artie wearily sank into the chair by the fire out of sight of his menacing self in the mirror. He picked up the stiff card signed only CEG in the delicate script Artie so adored. He allowed himself to breathe in the scent of the paper imagining her long fingers resting on the edge as she wrote. He was so miserably aware of how far away his dream of her was despite the short distance between them physically. Growing up beside her, Artie decided they would eventually marry. At eight years old, this idea had much certainty. He planned his entire life to accommodate this eventual marriage to his idol. At 21, he was daunted with the prospect of making his accepted rendition of this event a reality. The dream required so little. No action, no possibility of rejection or competition. In sleep and daydream, Lottie was automatically his: loving, compliant, and accepting with none of this awkward tension that made him so very tired.

Bolstered only by his sporadic and incomplete readings—sustained intellectual pursuits made him anxious—Artie instilled into his ardor for his childhood playmate what he sensed was an appropriate amount of drama.

"'Lottie,' he began again. 'My regard for you has always been high. And now it is...higher.' How pathetic." At a loss, he slumped further into the chair and sulked.

Artie, the dubious heir to Galveston's third wealthiest cotton dynasty, left his mansion for that of his dearest object, dressed finally, but no more sure how to propose to Lottie at her impromptu picnic than he had been for the last six months when he first determined he would screw up his courage to transfer the dream he had nurtured for over a decade into a reality.

13.   Anxiety

Cast all your anxiety on him because he cares for you. 1
Peter 5:7

Tom surprised himself with how soundly he slept that night. He had romantically assumed he would never be able to relax enough from the day's unusual excitement and thus would pace the floor in passionate agitation. Contrary to this overactive imagination, Tom read for a few hours after dinner and was pleasantly interrupted from this occupation when the hotel's man-of-all-work knocked on his room door softly to deliver a note. Improbable as the conjecture may have been, he momentarily hoped it was another note from Lottie, but was not in the least disappointed to discover a few lines from Liam. He wrote only briefly—Tom wondered if he were being monitored but dismissed that thought as uncharitable. Regardless, Liam's words were unmistakably supportive, kind, and joyful. He mentioned seeing Lottie and Tom at Cashlin the next day. Tom looked forward to receiving his blessing and discussing the future with this friend and mentor.

After reading Liam's uplifting note and rereading Lottie's priceless script several more times as if he might be tested on the exact wording, Tom slept soundly, experiencing the most incredibly sweet dreams of my life. All of the scenes starred Lottie, but one was especially memorable. In it, Lottie wore a flowing white gown that reminded Tom of Helen's marble dress he'd called to memory from the afternoon's comparisons. She was walking on the beach with several unfamiliar children. Tom kept trying to reach her before she dragged the folds of her dress in the waves. Every time it seemed to be too close, she would look back over her shoulder and flash an enchanting, unearthly smile directly at the speechless Tom – then it would start over again and again.

Dawn's eerie light woke Tom Saturday as it slanted through the small window, and he fairly leapt from his unfamiliar bed. Despite what seemed like an entire night's worth of dreaming, he woke refreshed and eager to commence this day. Even with deliberate stalling, Tom was ready hours before he could possibly arrive at Cashlin with any sense of propriety. He decided to walk to the beach so prominent in his captivating dreams. The day would end in rain, Tom predicted, gauging by the wind and the feel of the air on the open beach.

Tom typically paid more attention to changes in weather, but had been rather preoccupied these several days and weeks and had not noticed any sign of this storm's coming. Even in Boston, storms were so common up and down the coast all through summer,

Tom wasn't surprised but did utter a quick prayer that the rain would delay enough to at least go through the motions at Lottie's fabricated picnic knowing she would have put forth significant effort even for a façade.

"But I don't really care," Tom thought smugly. "Even if we end up eating on blankets in the huge ballroom instead of on the lawn, I get to hear Lottie again soon."

Having never expected her to return his love, Tom hadn't prepared to visualize these beautiful images and make all these lovely mental plans about their future together. Funny how we limit dreams. Tom could only marvel at her seemingly instantaneous connection to him with intense gratitude. An admired friend who would now become an esteemed and adored wife.

Tom thought, "Me with a wife! Amazing!" Tom never stopped to think a more typical courtship may have been more gradual, slower—a comfortable familiarity that sighs into a stronger emotion cementing a lasting connection. That pattern didn't compare to their situation, and yet Tom knew they too had passed through similar phases; they simply accelerated the pace. Tom understood we would need to perform a show of sorts that mimicked this more traditional wooing because others would not be able to understand how they could know our minds so soon after meeting. Tom supposed many onlookers would think them impetuous and foolhardy, drunk with a transitory passion that would tire them both and push them into premature decisions about which the young couple would regret not seeking wiser council.

Once Tom had met Lottie and allowed himself to absorb this mystifying idea of being always one with her, he realized Lottie was what he had been searching for all along. She personified the single idea around which all his other thoughts revolved, and had been revolving for years. had been forcing other ideas into focus; trying on plans others had for him as if trying to make a too-small shoe fit. But nothing had felt this right—been this right. No other town. No other person. No other plan. Not even his mother's long-cherished, guilt-heavy dream of Tom becoming a priest—a choice that he had determined even before he realized he loved Lottie was not the way he would honor God. Tom understood now that God had not called me to serve in that way. He had orchestrated all of this, and He was glad. Tom would eventually have to figure out why his mother had been so adamant, giving him no chance to decide his own route, and reconcile her to his decision to abandon her long-held plans.

Tom gathered strength in knowing he and Lottie were such kindred spirits and that facing challenges would be much easier together than alone. Hypothetically, had Lottie not embraced the truth of their love, which of course, is the part that makes it hypothetical because had she not, she wouldn't be Lottie. Despite this unalterable truth, Tom know he could have survived in body. He understood clearly that she didn't just accept Tom as her partner; she recognized that their togetherness was part of their innermost beings. So, had some force intervened to keep us asunder, as does occasionally and sadly occur between one spirit lodged in two bodies, Tom would have physically survived, but he knew he would not be whole. That's how Tom explained to himself at least how totally at ease he was about his immediate and total connection to Lottie. He had no ordinary young lover's anxiety that she may change her mind or petulantly decide to trifle with his affections. He felt no jealousy of her past or worries over her present relations with others. Tom would meld into those as she would seamlessly blend into his small world. They were both eagerly anticipating the joy of knowing each other more fully in a way only time and their togetherness could effect, but they were far and away beyond any trepidation concerning the constancy of their now stated affections. Tom often reminded himself that he didn't deserve such grace from God while in the same breath knowing without a doubt this love and union came directly from Him.

Soon though—not today, of course—today was for celebrating, but one day soon, Tom could see how he would have to force himself to become much more disciplined to accomplish anything more than contentedly contemplating God's handiwork in Lottie's perfection. He wondered if her actual presence in his daily life would help him in this regard or further hinder his resolve.

As if on cue, a howling wind on the beach stirred and echoed enough to make Tom look up from his reveries. No rain yet, just wind—a loud, insistent wind—but the rain was indeed on its way. Looking out into the Gulf, Tom could see the thick wall of dark clouds hovering on the horizon. They would have no cheery picnic weather this day. Knowing he was still woefully early, Tom bent his eager steps toward Cashlin stopping at The Upper Crust, the tiny German bakery Liam loved so well from their rambles. Armed with Mrs. Coverdale's linzer cookies as his delicious albeit measly contribution to the feast, Tom moved toward Lottie as if traversing a path of magnetized sunshine despite the strong wind that tousled his hair and challenged his balance.

Tom had rarely seen Cashlin completely quiet. Someone was always tending to the minutia of maintaining the large estate, but today when Tom approached the kitchen entrance, assuming the privilege of an intimate friend, he found less bustle than he had expected. Tom had guessed he would encounter at the least some debate ensuing about the probability of moving the preparations indoors. A few tables had been erected close to the buildings, but he saw no other evidence of an upcoming event. Confused, Tom moved to check his father's parting gift, the old timepiece in his vest pocket—fearful he was even earlier than he had estimated. At that moment, Tom came upon y Lottie walking out the door striding purposefully into the yard. Struck again by her actual beauty dimmed so pathetically in his mind's eye, Tom did happen to note she was closely followed by several servants and a handful of others, obviously guests assembled for the ill-fated picnic. Tom couldn't mistake that Lottie's eyes brightened on discovering him unexpectedly so close to the door. What an infinitesimal detail to notice, but oh, how it charmed him!

Lottie smiled slightly, nodding at Tom and spoke for the benefit of the others in greeting him, "Ah, Mr. McDermott."

Taking her lead in our complicity, with a thrill Tom couldn't repress totally, he replied, "Miss Gallagher—what a delightful idea you had."

"Thank you for coming, Mr. McDermott. I'm not sure my timing was the best though. Robert is very concerned about this weather. He's a bit of a worrier, but I do admit he's usually correct." She looked up at the sky as she spoke as if to assess for herself.

"We can still do our best," Tom responded trying his utmost not to stare and to be social to the few other guests who had arrived as early as he had; Artie Morgan was there, of course. His eyes had not brightened upon first discovering Tom's presence.

Lottie's father was not home Tom quickly learned, away on business again, which seemed a sensitive point with Lottie. Tom would have to learn all of her sensitivities. He had especially hoped to speak with Mr. Gallagher today privately to secure his permission to court Lottie properly. Tom would suffer no rumors spreading because he had rushed any public demonstration of his regard.

As Tom had guessed, the group had come outside to verify Robert's pessimistic assessment of the ominous storm, although he did not see the quiet butler among them. The servants looked to Lottie for guidance, waiting patiently for whatever she decided would be the course of action.

In a subtle move that delighted Tom because it was one of many firsts for them, Lottie looked to Tom for advice on this simple matter. She quite obviously was well able to direct her own servants and certainly had more experience doing so than he did, but her deliberate deference to his opinion made Tom feel as though we were already making decisions together—as a couple. No one master, and yet no side slighted either. Tom noticed one or two others of the gathered party noticed the shift as well.

With sincere gratitude for being treated with such respect, Tom quietly accepted Lottie's offering noting, "Miss Gallagher, I was just now at the beach, and I am afraid Robert is correct. A storm is certainly brewing today. How strong I can't tell."

Lottie frowned slightly in light of their frustrated pleasantries, Tom assumed, and he continued, "We might make do in a cozy room indoors for our picnic if the rain and wind deny us our first choice, mightn't we?"

Artie spoke first in a very formal tone as if to an underling or idiot, Tom couldn't tell which he intended to imply, "Mr. McDermott, quite obviously you are unfamiliar with this social tradition, but eating outside in amenable meteorological conditions is the whole purpose of conducting a picnic. Perhaps we should delay to another time, Charlotte. The others may be able to reach home before the rain if they leave now."

As if oblivious to the intended snub toward Tom or the veiled connection he forged between the two of them, Lottie said, "It just seems such a waste," as she continued watching Tom, "especially after we've waited patiently so long."

Tom hoped he wasn't blushing, but loved the feeling of our conspiratorial hidden agenda. Turning quickly to Mary Ellen and Sarah, her cook, Lottie asked, "Surely can manage inside, can we not, Mary Ellen? Cook was such a dear to make so many of my favorites. Come. I'll help you spread blankets up in the old nursery. We can spoil nothing in that barn of a room."

So saying, the three women turned to re-enter the house to prepare for this change in plans. Artie tried to compose himself at having his idea summarily ignored. Quite graciously, Tom didn't even smile at his victory over Artie.

The women began finding the items that would help Lottie serve her guests in an appropriate style despite this Bohemian change. They were surprised by very few of Lottie's requests and daunted by none. They loved her so well regardless, her every wish was always attended with sincere alacrity.

The guests even joined in with what Lottie promised the children would be "great fun." Mrs. Laraby and her two young sons seemed very comfortable moving old furniture out of the way and spreading the pile of blankets out on our makeshift picnic area at the top of the house. Artie seemed to realize peevishness would gain him no advantage or favorable attention and thus he cooperated to remain part of the cheerful group. The boys carried innumerable baskets and platters of foods of all sorts at Cook's direction, sneaking bites at every chance. The maternal Mary Ellen seemed entranced at entertaining the small boys having only adult charges at Cashlin now.

Just moments after they all sat down to enjoy the picnic lunch amidst laughter and teasing, Father Liam came quickly up the stairs into the party. He was followed closely behind by Robert who looked uncharacteristically windblown and flushed with exertion.

Robert quickly said, "Miss Lottie, I am sorry to interrupt your party, but the storm is even worse than I thought this morning."

Lottie stood with Tom as the men entered. She looked at the anxious expressions on both of their faces and spoke calmly, "Father Liam, Robert, how bad is it then? We haven't had even a little rain since yesterday afternoon. Last night I sat outside reading until dark without a drop."

"I'm afraid Robert is right again, Dear," Liam greeted Lottie with a kiss, "despite our calm lead up to it. This one appears to be serious, and you know how well our Robert can predict these things."

Father Liam moved to shake Tom's hand and smiled warmly, conveying volumes but saying nothing.

Robert blushed at Father Liam's praise, but then became somber in a moment. "Perhaps this will end up being just another overflow—they're terribly inconvenient and leave a dreadful mess, but no occasion for undue alarm certainly. I need to secure a few items in the garden, Miss Lottie. And everyone should make haste to arrive home to tend to closing their own shutters as fast as they can."

If nothing else, his tone of only slightly controlled panic spurred the group into action. Tom spoke at once without thinking of his changed condition at St. Patrick's, "I'll help Robert and then come to you at church, Father. We should be able to move all the benches and statues into the back lean-to without any trouble."

Artie stood now, "I can help here, Mr. McDermott, you go along and help at church."

Not wanting to waste time arguing, Tom was about to concede knowing he would double back here promptly when Father Liam spoke with a decided tone of authority that outranked us all. "Thank you both, Gentlemen. I did come here expressly to find help with this task knowing you to be here for the festivities. Artie, you come with me, then you'll be closer to home when we're done to help there. Tom, you and Robert should be able to manage here alone. Mrs. Laraby, is your servant here to drive you and the children home?"

"No, Father," Mrs. Laraby spoke sounding very young and frightened. "I sent him home early this morning. He won't be expecting to come this way for ever so long—hours and hours surely. I had no earthly idea anything like this would ruin our happy day. I declare, I just told Mr. Laraby last week how I do hate these summer storms. They were just as bad at home in Mobile. And I did hope I could outrun them coming here to Galveston as we did."

Lottie sweetly stemmed her flow of words, "Elly, you and the boys stay here for the afternoon. This will soon blow over, and there's no reason for you to chance ruining your lovely gown in the rain. Thank you Father Liam and Robert. We'll just have to reschedule our picnic. Do let's make all safe downstairs. Robert, you'll check on sweet Mrs. Kelsey across the way as well, please? She'll be frightened by the strong winds. Bring her here if you can persuade her."

Father Liam smiled at her adept diplomacy, calming present fears, anticipating future ones. He spoke quietly to her as he turned to leave, and Tom thought he heard, "so happy" but would have to wait until later to be sure. Liam walked out with Tom, purposefully taking his aside to say, "My dear friend—I take it you told her then?"

Tom smiled at his friend's keen interest with all the chaos around them, and answered in all-consuming joy, "I guess we actually told each other more or less. I couldn't be happier."

"It shows," he smiled. "I can't tell you how pleased I am. I didn't think it possible, but she's even more beautiful now than even just a few days hence. She's positively glowing. Promise me we'll talk soon, and I can hear all your plans."

Artie reluctantly left with Father Liam, and the children returned to their interrupted meals while Tom turned back to Robert who was speaking with Lottie.

Lottie spoke quietly, "Of course Bridget may stay down in the kitchen if she wishes, but she must stay here with us, Robert. Let me hear no more nonsense of her attempting to take Susie to her mother's in this wind. It's simply too far for both of them. And I wish Collette were here with them."

"I hate to impose, Miss Lottie," Robert looked torn knowing the two men must hurry with their work, "but for the storm, you know I would never have brought her here to Cashlin. I saw her trying to make it back from her employer's while I was out checking on the tides."

"Mr. McDermott, please help me convince Robert of my sincerity. He shouldn't send his niece Bridget and her baby out in this weather, should he?"

"I'm sure she'll be safe here until the wind dies down, Robert. It shouldn't be too long," Tom answered, seeing in Robert's downcast face that he didn't understand the whole situation.

"Yes, Sir," Robert replied without meeting Tom's eyes, "thank you for your concern."

Tom looked to Lottie to discern if she could help him understand quickly enough to be of any real help without wasting precious time.

Evidently, she decided she could not explain sufficiently without taking more time than they had at hand because she gently took over in a manner Tom cherished as she displayed her skill in nurturing and leading. She spoke quietly but firmly so only Robert and Tom could hear her but not such that we could not mistake her intention that Robert take her message as a mandated request to a servant from his mistress. Ignoring Robert's reluctance and taking advantage of the need for haste, Lottie said, "Robert, we must hurry; I insist you send Bridget here to me while you work outside with Mr. McDermott. I'll need her assistance with my guests, and the boys will delight in playing with the baby. Go on now."

Robert allowed himself the slightest glance at his generous mistress and mouthed, "Thank you."

Lottie whispered back, "Robert, please never forget, you are family to me. Bridget is like a sister, and she will always be welcomed in my home. No matter what. You need to remind her of that as well; it's been entirely too long since I've held our precious Susie."

The men turned to leave, and Robert's whole stance was altered. He instantly had more energy in his stride and seemed to have lost his timidity and anxiety. Lottie's goodness evidently had a broad, sweeping influence Tom was only just beginning to see.

Robert and Tom finished their tasks easily. Cashlin was so meticulously maintained, Robert was well able to organize the operation efficiently and in a manner that suited his detail-oriented mentality. He knew exactly what needed to be done to secure any loose objects against the potential of strong winds and excessive rains. With Tom's help, Robert was able to expedite the necessary preparations in far less time than Tom had expected.

14. Faith

I tell you the truth, if you have faith as small as a mustard seed, you can say to this mountain, 'Move from here to there' and it will move. Nothing will be impossible for you.

Matthew 17:19-21

Trying to prioritize the random thoughts battling his mind, Liam realized his young friend was not just suffering from the romantic slight he had recently experienced. Artie was scared. Liam forced his thoughts to focus. Should he too fear this unknown storm? His faith said no, but he realized a shudder spasmed down his back as the idea entered his mind.

Liam slowed his pace and reached his hand out to stop Artie's progress. He smiled once he had the young man's attention and leaned close to be heard over the wind, "You'll be fine once you get home, Son. It won't take too long to secure the items outside the church. I can do it myself if you want to head straight home."

Artie seemed relieved just to hear another's voice, "No, Father. I'm fine. I don't want you to do it all alone. This wind is just so strong. Father? You don't think it's really going to be so bad, do you? I mean, we've had summer storms before, but I've never felt wind like this."

"Me either," Liam answered as he started walking toward the churchyard again. They were in sight of the tall bell tower now. "God will protect us, but I'm afraid this one will be a little different, Artie."

Artie forced a laugh that sounded terribly out of place, and said, "Well, old St. Pat's doesn't look like it's afraid of any storm." Liam smiled and nodded.

The imposing stone structure of the old church with its rustic tower did indeed seem impenetrable. Faith undaunted in the face of adversity. The trees all around the main church structure swayed with an erratic rhythm as if the wind could ill-determine a set course. One blast would strike from the coast side and then abruptly, the swirling, hot air would shift and come down on the hapless trees and bushes surrounding St. Patrick's, punishing its audacity in not fleeing before this behemoth. Some limbs had already succumbed to the powerful force, and displaced leaves were floating through the air like confetti. "God will see us all through" Liam again assured himself no less than Artie. They quickly grasped for some small benches, statues, and signage.

"You should head home," Liam urged Artie. "Your folks will be concerned. After this is over, let me know how you and your family fared. Thank you for helping me here." As if he hadn't heard a word of

Liam's farewell, Artie looked up and asked, "He isn't going to become a priest, is he?"

As incongruent as the thought appeared, as inappropriate as the topic seemed in the face of the increasing ferocity of the storm, Liam understood completely. Deciding raw and complete honesty, painful as it may be, would be the most expedient approach with so many other emergencies facing them, Liam nodded and said, "You're right. I don't think Tom will take Holy Orders, Artie. I'll guess he didn't even know that until yesterday. Lottie is wonderful, Artie. And I know you two have been friends for a long time. But you will find the woman God created especially for you. Trust that He is in control. Even when it hurts. Now hurry home, and we can talk more about this later when we know everyone is safe." Artie nodded, still looking as if he were trying to determine the answer to a particularly difficult equation. He put his face down as he ran into the wind toward his father's mansion.

Liam watched the young man's diminishing figure and paused to reflect on the irony his broken heart presented. Artie would always remember his perceived loss of Lottie in connection with his memories of this momentous storm. Unconnected, unintentional, yet locked forever in his mind. "I wonder how much all of us will mark events in reference to this storm for the rest of our lives," Liam said to himself as he carefully drug small statues of the Sacred Heart and the Blessed Virgin Mary too heavy to lift into the back alcove to a safer nook on the porch.

For the next hour as the winds shook the trees over his head, Father Liam undertook the manual tasks of securing any lightweight items outside the church building while he prayed silently for his friends and parishioners.

Father O'Mallary and their elderly servant Sean were busily working inside the church protecting the Blessed Sacrament and the more delicate decorations that could be removed from the walls. Liam lifted the large wooden cross beam onto the brackets securing the church door behind him as the two older men were finishing. Liam urged them both into the shallow tunnel that led the short distance to the cellar of the old rectory. It wasn't truly a basement because the island wouldn't support a true underground structure at sea level, but the original priests who oversaw the construction of the parish located the church and priests' residence on high ground and established this little known connecting footpath. It was more a convenience during inclement weather than a security measure, but Liam liked the Old World mystique of it. He used the passage far more often than Father

O'Mallary who disliked the low ceiling and the dimly lit passage.

Today though, Father O'Mallary didn't argue with Liam's idea to get the men quickly back to the relative safety of the old rectory. Sean had set the outside shutters against the tall windows as soon as the wind had started bending the trees a few hours before. Having lived in Galveston longer than either of the priests, Sean performed storm preparations by rote understanding as islanders seem to intuit that whether the storm were big or small, any work he could finish before the storm hit would save days of repair work afterwards. To a servant, a storm was a much more practical affair. Year in and year out, Sean had watched storm clouds scuttle over the familiar beaches of the shore, promising a few hours of suspended work after the scurry to tie down as much of the outside decorations as possible. Sean took this storm in quiet, calm stride, which soothed Liam's anxious nerves. Liam was amazed that it had only been a few hours since he'd left the church to join his friends for the last picnic of summer. How he prayed they would be safe during this tempest.

Liam settled down with Father O'Mallary, Sean, and the two ancient house cats in the innermost room of the old rectory. He had assisted Sean in moving the settee from its place near the window to the middle of the room. The elderly priest routinely napped here of an afternoon, and Liam helped the old man settle into the comfortable spot in an effort to allay the mounting fears as the sounds of the storm increased outside.

Almost immediately, Father O'Mallary fell into a deep slumber snoring in cadence with the loud ticking of the mantle clock. Sean had asked Liam if the young priest required any additional service numerous times until Liam said, "Sean, thank you for your kind offers of assistance. I'm sure I am fine. Please rest yourself as well. I think it best if we remain all together, but I'm afraid we're in for a rather long night. You need not feel you are on duty constantly...well, until Father O'Mallary wakes anyway." Liam smiled at the servant.

"Thank you, Sir," Sean smiled and nodded looking over at the sleeping priest. "I fear you are correct. Do you mind if I continue reading Mr. Melville's story—it seems right just now?"

"Yes, indeed," Liam laughed gently. "Moby Dick does seem appropriate. I haven't read that in years. Of course, you know you are welcome to any volume in the library at any time. I think I'll stick with my friend Jane—'there was no possibility of taking a walk that day' here either."

"Thank you, Sir," Liam answered retreating to a corner with his leviathan as Liam entered the bleakness of the English countryside.

15. Hope

Religion that God our Father accepts as pure and faultless is this: to look after orphans and widows in their distress and to keep oneself from being polluted by the world. James 1:26-27

William brought the last stack of blankets up the kitchen staircase at the back of the orphanage. Mother Superior had asked William and two other older boys, Frank and Albert, to carry most of the supplies up to the top floor while the sisters took the younger children into the communal dining room of the new Girls' Dormitory building on the second floor. The Boys' Dormitory was slightly larger, but it was older and sometimes leaked in heavy rain; the sisters were determined to keep their charges safe and sound as they rode out this fierce storm. Mother Superior didn't want to frighten the children even more than they already were during the storm. She instructed the sisters to have the children singing cheerful praise songs to Mary. The children knew their favorite by heart and sang loudly:

Queen of the Waves, look forth across the ocean
From north to south, from east to stormy west,
See how the waters with tumultuous motion
Rise up and foam without a pause or rest.
But fear we not, tho' storm clouds round us gather,

Thou art our Mother and thy little Child

Is the All Merciful, our loving Brother

God of the sea and of the tempest wild.

Help, then sweet Queen, in our exceeding danger,

By thy seven griefs, in pity Lady save;

Think of the Babe that slept within the manger

And help us now, dear Lady of the Wave.

Up to thy shrine we look and see the glimmer

Thy votive lamp sheds down on us afar;

Light of our eyes, oh let it ne'er grow dimmer,

Till in the sky we hail the morning star.

Then joyful hearts shall kneel around thine altar

And grateful psalms re-echo down the nave;

Never our faith in thy sweet power can falter,

Mother of God, our Lady of the Wave.

William could hear the muffled voices through the floor below as he dropped his burden. Standing back up to his full height, he peered out the window toward the churning Gulf. He started humming the tune from downstairs just to rid his mind of the noise outside. He couldn't see the shore line, but even without the typical reference points, he could see the waves were rougher and higher than they should be. As he stood and stared at the coming storm, William heard Sister Bernadette, his favorite teacher, as she climbed the stairs and called his name.

"Here you are, lad," Sister Bernadette said as she stopped to catch her breath after her quick climb. "You've done a fine job, Wills. Thank you."

William smiled shyly and asked, "Does Mother need me to bring anything else up here, Sister?"

"No," Sister Bernadette said, looking around the sparsely furnished area. "She would like the long clothesline rope we use for our outings with the little ones. Have you seen that?"

"Sure," William nodded. "It's over in the storage shed. I can run get it." William moved toward the stairwell.

"Oh, Wills, I don't think you should," Sister Bernadette walked over to the window. The rain hadn't started yet, but Bernadette could feel it hanging heavily in the air. She shivered but knew the room wasn't cold. She said, "The wind is so fierce."

"It's not too bad yet," William answered starting down the stairs. "I can get over there and back before the rain starts. You'll see."

Bernadette smiled at the retreating teen as he ran down the steep stairs. More than the others for some reason, the boy reminded her of the gangly brothers she missed so from her home in Ohio. "Do hurry, lad," she whispered to the empty chamber.

16. Love

I would hurry to my place of shelter, far from the tempest and storm. Psalm 55:7-9

Once finished outside, Robert and Tom returned to the house, noting the wind was increasing and rain was falling in intermittent bursts.

Lottie had moved the remnant guests downstairs to a more comfortable room, and Bridget's baby was fast asleep on a soft chair in the middle of the vast room. The older boys were working a large picture puzzle on a table by the far wall with Lottie and Mrs. Laraby. The boys' mother looked bored, but Lottie seemed lost in concentration looking for a piece to match the one in her hand.

Speaking quietly to not disturb the pleasant domestic scene Tom said to Lottie, "This obstinate storm seems determined to come!"

"Determination can be an excellent quality," she said still looking at the mass of tiny shapes on the table, "but I do hope we don't receive too much rain this time. The lawn was such a mess from the last storm. Do you remember, Bridget?"

The young girl smiled shyly and nodded.

After a few minutes, Tom spoke quietly again to Lottie as they walked toward the sliding panel door into the hall, "I'm going to check on Father Liam and see what I can find out about the storm. The wind keeps getting stronger. Mrs. Laraby and the boys shouldn't try to leave—well, everyone really. Can you make arrangements for them all to stay the night if it comes to that? It's so dark already, and it's only mid-afternoon."

Looking more concerned than before, but keeping her voice calm, Lottie said, "Of course. We'll begin working on it immediately; we have plenty of room."

"Good. I'll feel better knowing you're all safe," Tom responded.

Before he could turn to leave, Lottie touched Tom's arm, as if he needed any physical contact to direct his entire attention to her. She spoke so earnestly, he was moved, "But...you'll come back, won't you, Tom? Please?"

He replied, "We may have to stay inside for some time until this blows over. Are you sure...? What I mean is...your father. He may not approve of my being here...overnight."

Lottie looked directly at Tom, suddenly realizing his concern. She blushed beautifully, but composed herself saying, "I'm sure Papa would approve of anyone I felt...so comfortable with." She paused and seemed to consider something for a moment. "That won't be an issue. If…if you want to come back, of course."

Tom looked deeply into her incredible eyes allowing the love shining there to wash over and calm him in the midst of her anxiety about this curious social situation in which they found themselves. They were speaking volumes to each other without words. The pacing of this nascent courtship outstripped any previous experience with which either of them had any familiarity. Almost dizzy with the passion buffeting him from her earnest eyes, Tom resolved the quandary and said, "I just want to make sure Liam doesn't need more help at St. Pat's. I'll be back as quickly as I can."

17.   Storm

When the storm has swept by, the wicked are gone, but the righteous stand firm forever. Proverbs 10:24-26

When Tom returned from the church and the preparations Father Liam efficiently coordinated, Cashlin was full of life. The wind was blowing more strongly than when he had left, but it was not yet fierce. They all sensed it would eventually be far worse. The vibrant colors in the early afternoon sky were what made the scene eerie, ominously predicting some unknown activity in the near future. All around him in the short distance he covered, he encountered residents securing yard ornaments and bringing in porch furniture. Storms were part of island life, and Galveston knew how to prepare. The difference today was the urgency with which people moved about their unexpected but necessary tasks. This storm had come with no warning, changing the blue skies to black in hours.

Lottie directed Mary Ellen and Robert to prepare two guest rooms for Mrs. Laraby and her children. Tom was to be housed in her absent brother's room. Bridget and the baby could share Lottie's suite while the servants occupied their own rooms at the top of the commodious house. Lottie also asked Sarah to prepare more food for us all, and Robert and Mary

Ellen were gathering extra candles and lamps for the early darkness. In her orderly fashion, Lottie had delegated tasks for everyone, even the children, to occupy their minds away from the coming storm. She had endured several tropical storms growing up on the island and knew the worst part for many was the noise of the howling wind. Lottie promised the boys, "we'll would sing and play the piano to try to be louder!"

She had no unusual fear for this storm, but was anxious for us all to be safely indoors as the storm approached.

She took Tom slightly away from the others as soon as he returned, motioning for Robert to join them. "Robert, Mr. McDermott, how does it look?" she asked when she knew the others couldn't hear.

"The wind is certainly stronger since I left," Tom began, "and the water at the beach was choppy even this morning before I arrived for the picnic."

Robert agreed, "I tried to get to the weather office this morning when I was out, but no one was there. I'm afraid we'll have rain enough and wind to drive the waves inland a bit with this storm. Mr. Cline hoisted the flags on the Levy Building. It was the red flag with a black square and a white flag on top. It's been a few years since we've this large of a storm brewing. We may even have flood water closer to the shore, Miss Lottie."

Lottie looked worried and lost in thought. "Those poor dears close to the beach! I do wish we had a bit more time, but it feels as if the rain is soon to be on us. Robert, could you and Mr. McDermott fasten all the shutters before the rain begins please?"

"Of course," he replied, embarrassed he'd not thought to do so before.

"I know it will make the house darker, but there's no help for it. The children won't be as frightened once we're all together, and they have Sarah's delightful cakes to eat," she replied.

"I do wish we could fetch the sisters and the children up from St. Mary's," she continued. "Sweet angels! The wee ones will be so scared. Your first big storm is always the worst, but this may end up being all bark and no bite, too. We'll check on them first thing when this passes through. And I know Liam won't leave St. Pat's. For once, I'm glad Papa didn't make it home; he'll be safe in Houston."

Tom looked at her with a mixture of awe and respect for her calm, generous nature thinking of all those dear to her. He promised, "I'll help Robert with the windows now and be ready for whatever else I can do. I'm not sure if this will be much like a Boston blizzard, but just let me know how to help."

She beamed at Tom as if they were comrades in arms. She spoke softly, only to him, saying, "Thank you so much, Tom. I feel better having you here. Fortunately, we'll have plenty of time to have our postponed talk—I can never sleep during storms. Mary Ellen tells me Mama and Papa met during a storm in New Orleans. Anyway, you never forget your first big storm."

He smiled and said, "I'm sure I won't want to."

Then in a moment, she assumed her leader's mantle again and announced she would meet them back inside, "I simply *must* convince dear old Mrs. Hoglen across the way that I need her to be with us, poor thing. Mrs. Kelsey wouldn't budge when Robert asked her earlier. I'll try once more. Neither of the dears will ever admit to any fear!" She was down the wide porch steps before Robert or Tom could stop her, hair whipping in the gusts, so they turned to begin the relatively easy task of moving the tall shutters in place to protect the many windows of the mansion.

They both looked toward her voice as Lottie shouted over the wind, "Mr. Miller, is that you? Mrs. Miller? Why are you so far from home with the children?"

Robert and Tom left their task momentarily to discover what Lottie had found.

The Millers were one of many influential Black families who lived on the far eastern section of the island. Lottie helped Sheryl at St. Patrick's with the children's catechism program. Warren Miller had established the first Black newspaper in Galveston the year Daniel had arrived, and they had been good friends since, both ambitious, intelligent, and amiable. His first wife had died many years previously, and his marriage to his new, young wife Sheryl had pleased Daniel and Lottie immensely.

"Oh, Charlotte, dear!" Sheryl spoke over the increasing roar of wind. "I couldn't wait for Warren to return home. He was just going to secure the shutters at the newspaper office, but I couldn't wait any longer. Then I tried to call, but the phone line was dead. I know it was foolish of me."

"Nonsense, Sheryl," Lottie spoke with concern. "But I won't hear of you trying to make it home in this gale! Little Charlie, my buddy, will be blown into the sky like a kite!" She smiled at the frightened young boy who peered at her from behind his father's legs.

As one who rarely brooks refusal, she took them both by the elbows and ushered them up the porch steps. Seeing Tom near, she quickly introduced the newcomers as if this were a pleasant social gathering and then stopped any potential argument asking, "Mr. Miller, could you please assist Mr. McDermott with these last shutters while I steal Robert to help me persuade our elderly neighbor to join us? Believe it or not, this was supposed to be a picnic! Sheryl, take the babies inside quickly. And Charlie, you find Miss Mary Ellen and tell her you need a cookie."

And as fast as the mesmerizing buzz of her words, Lottie was gone having added four souls to the ranks with Robert in tow to procure even more.

Once together again, Lottie had the entire group sit down to a lovely, relaxed meal. Even though it was only mid-afternoon, the candles and oil lamps were lit against the darkening sky and the shuttered windows. Had they been able to ignore the howl of the wind, they could easily have supposed this to be a carefree party of friends. Lottie hosted such events frequently, and the adults tried to enjoy the hospitality Lottie offered to allay the growing concern for the strange weather.

Tom had overheard Lottie's earlier directions to Sarah to be sure to over-prepare so the group would have more food for later during the storm and to include all the guests and the three permanent servants as well as Robert's niece Bridget in the count for mouths to feed. Lottie's thorough solicitude always included her beloved family of servants, and she never tried to emphasize their subservient position by cutting corners at their expense.

After the group ate and Mary Ellen had cleared away the dishes, Tom went down to Robert in the kitchen on the ground floor. It was a comfortable, large room at the back of the house, with food storage areas and preparation stations around a central work area. Tom stood in awe at the sheer space, knowing it was not used at anywhere near capacity for this small family. Robert looked relieved to see Tom as he walked in the half-door and bolted it against the wind behind him.

"Mr. Tom," he exclaimed, short of breath. "The storm's growing worse each time I go out. I wish I could see the Gulf, then I'd know for sure what to expect."

Tom wasn't quite sure what good that would do since the storm would come regardless of their knowing anything about the state of the water. But he, too, was struggling to be in some way helpful or at least active in this tense time.

"Perhaps the cupola would allow us a tall enough vantage," Tom said, remembering the ornamental glass dome at the highest point of the mansion. "We can't possibly go on the roof in this wind; is that accessible from inside?"

Eagerly, Mary Ellen spoke first, "Aye. The children used to play there. But I daresay it hasn't been opened since they were wee ones."

"Let's try to get there," Tom said to Robert as the young man moved toward the door again. "Mary Ellen, please tell Lottie our plans without the others hearing. I believe they're singing in the parlor."

"Yes, Mr. Tom," she replied affably, and he realized for the second time since he had entered the kitchen that she too accepted his newly formed position of authority without question or rancor; Tom was an ally with Lottie in this time of crisis, and they approved.

"Robert," Tom asked. "Do you know how to reach the cupola?"

Before he could speak, Mary Ellen again answered briskly as if any delay brought with it entirely too much anxiety. "Robert, dear, it's easiest through the attic entrance in Miss Lottie's room behind the rocker." She smiled fondly at Robert who seemed at a momentary loss for words.

Robert nodded, and Tom thrilled at the prospect of seeing Lottie's room even as he checked himself to remember the severity of the situation. This day was changing drastically with every minute; Tom had no idea how it would end.

Her private chambers were as graceful and serene as Tom expected them to be as a reflection of her, in soft greens and dusty rose pinks covering the walls and furnishings. Tom noticed many books and a violin propped on a meticulously carved music stand as Robert quickly ushered him through the spacious room. Tom wondered again in a fraction of a moment how he could possibly think of anything but the storm, but the appeal of knowing any small detail about Lottie he didn't already possess was overwhelming. The mind is a wondrous entity with its seemingly limitless ability to divide and process, catalog and analyze all in a momentary glance. The impending storm was becoming more and more threatening, and yet Tom sensed a tremendous peace throughout his whole being that he was where he should be. For the first time ever, he belonged. And God willing, this is where he would stay.

The men passed through to a narrow, steep stairwell, stark in comparison to the airy cheer evident in Lottie's quarters. The utilitarian, uncarpeted, and unfinished stairs opened to a large attic area filled with what appeared to be a room of ill-matched castoffs—an arm chair, a part of a bed frame, an upended table, dress forms waiting for ball gowns, a silent rocking horse ready for another race, and a large baby carriage lined one wall dimly lit from Robert's lantern and the faint light issuing from their destination. Boxes and stacks of various-sized containers seemed haphazardly placed in the large storage area, monuments to all people keep without rational explanation—too precious to lose forever, too significant to resign entirely.

They reached the cupola by mounting a ladder at the far end of the attic space. The dome consisted of a glass encased enclosure with a small foot ledge and narrow bench running around the base. The men were able to stand up without hitting their heads, but just barely. They could understand why Lottie and Patrick would love to play here—not only was its size much more suitable to children, but also the views all around were breathtaking. Tom tried to determine how high he was, counting the many staircases they had covered to arrive here high above the island. Would this be three stories or four? He couldn't decide and was on the point of asking Robert. Then Tom turned and was momentarily stunned by the beauty of the view—the raw power in the sky, the unearthly colors all around. As he did when Tom first stepped into Lottie's personal chambers, he knew nothing but the awe-inspiring magnitude of the vista—until Robert's gasp reminded Tom of their purpose.

"Look, Sir," Robert pointed at the beach, and Tom instantly understood the terror in his voice.

The typically gentle rolling waves of the Gulf's shore had turned into a monstrous beast throwing anger at the sand as walls of grey foaming water churned and crashed at the shoreline. The screaming wind pushed the water far beyond what they both knew to be the sands of the recreational beach on pleasant summer days. For a few minutes, neither of them seemed to be able to realize what was wrong with the picture they were watching from this crow's nest so far inland.

As Tom looked at the distant beach—the same sandy shore he had walked this very morning in his joyful anticipation of seeing Lottie; or was that yesterday? Surely, this day had been going on longer than only a few hours? As he looked, Tom saw the water creep forward then retreat, creep forward then retreat. Or did it? The motion seemed unnatural—too fast and jerky in its execution to be graceful. If he hadn't known better, Tom might have guessed this were some comic optical illusion. Some child's toy gone awry. Then it hit him the water that came in such violent thrusts wasn't receding in its usual ebb and flow of universal cleansing. The water had nowhere else to go but didn't know what to do when it struck objects—

houses, fences, a street lamp. It obstinately hit and separated to move around the unrelenting obstacles, hissing its displeasure at being even momentarily stopped as it obeyed some internal urging to pulse forward. The ugly surge cruelly battered down the weaker forms it met; posts snapped cleanly; small trees bent awkwardly to the ground as if twigs with only a few bending back wearily in place to await the next onslaught. From their vantage point, the waves didn't even resemble water—it was a grey army crawling to demolish its enemy. The wind suddenly rose behind the troops and forced the ranks to their feet, encouraging the line forward, compelling the putty-colored mass to take up new fronts and strive for the next goal. Tom stared mesmerized, waiting for the water to turn back and flow to where it belonged. But the shuddering gray mass of water would allow no deployed waves back into her chaotic ranks. New lines of waves pounded furiously, unmercifully on the water attempting to retreat. Tom shook his head to clear the confusing images from his mind. What was happening? Robert and Tom had only been in the cupola for a few minutes, both in a separate but similar hell.

Tom looked at Robert and spoke quickly words neither of them wanted to admit. "Robert, the water's flooding the streets, but it isn't even raining yet."

"Yes, Sir," he replied automatically.

"Has it ever flooded this far inland, Robert?" Tom asked, dreading his answer.

"No, Sir," he answered sounding as relieved as Tom was for only a moment, but added nervously, "it hasn't since I've been here, which is before our Miss Lottie was born, but I've never seen it come so fast either."

Without debating any further, Tom decided to act and somehow knew Lottie would be with him in this decision. He delighted in that feeling of intrinsic communion more than he could express even inwardly and stored away the feeling to analyze later.

"Robert, we must move everyone upstairs. I truly don't think the water will rise even into the house, but this storm is more powerful than anything I've ever read about or seen. Go get Mary Ellen, Sarah, Bridget and the baby, and bring them all into the great hall downstairs—away from the large round window; we don't have time to secure that, I'm afraid. I'll gather Miss Gallagher and her guests. We'll need to cover the glass in Miss Gallagher's room as well. I saw the wood in the attic."

He nodded and they both turned to crawl down the ladder. Tom motioned for Robert to go first and thought to add, "And Robert, bring all the food the four of you can carry."

"Food, sir?" Robert looked puzzled, "we just ate."

"Yes, I'll come as well, as soon as I get word to the others," Tom explained. "We don't know how much time we have, and if we do have water coming in, it will flood the kitchen first. We must hurry, man." As they reached the bare flooring, a bolt of lightning filled the sky illuminating the entire attic with its sulfurous glow; then the sudden percussion of pelting rain seemed to punctuate Tom's urgency as Robert ran to do his bidding trusting the young man blindly.

The lightening flash coincided exactly with Cashlin's loss of electric power. The mansion had all the latest conveniences, including electric lights, but Lottie and the staff didn't use the lights often during the daytime hours since the large windows illuminated most of the rooms well without them. Today's dark skies would have been reason enough to have them on though.

"Isn't this an adventure, boys?" a still smiling Lottie asked Mattie and Luke, Mrs. Laraby's young sons, who were looking less enthusiastic about the day's events as the wind grew louder and the servants moved to light candles well above the reach of all the small children. "We'll pretend we're camping and it's the middle of the night!" Lottie's unflappable good spirits seemed to rouse everyone though, and she maintained an easy banter as the group gathered in the large room-sized hallway outside her own room and the other sleeping chambers on that floor.

Six-year-old Mattie was the first to fall victim to the fears no one else would mention aloud. Tears welling in his huge blue eyes, Mattie whined, "Oh Miss Lottie, I don't want to go camping. I want to go home now. I'm scared."

"Matthew!" Mrs. Laraby snapped, "You stop that crying and be a man." She seemed embarrassed and frazzled at not knowing how to stop her son from speaking so plainly and rudely, as a guest in another's home, without seeing the absurdity of worrying over a ludicrous social convention at such a time.

Lottie wanted neither to berate the frightened child further nor to embarrass her just-as-scared friend who was ill-equipped for spending so many uninterrupted hours with her sons unassisted.

"Mrs. Laraby," Tom softly asked her to bring down the noise level, "I wondered if I might tell the boys a story about a snow storm I once saw in Boston?"

"What's snow?" Mattie took the bait and wiped his eyes on the back of his hand as Lottie smiled at Tom and moved closer to her friend to lend her comforting presence to the anxious young mother. What Tom wouldn't do to receive the boon of Lottie's appreciative admiration would be hard to determine.

Each one of the fear-stretched faces, child and adult alike, seemed to look Tom's direction as his mind scrambled to tune out the present screech of wind and draw out the beauty of the gentle blanketing flakes. With nods from his listeners who would have been content with any topic that took them away from the unknown and unwelcome specter angrily demanding attention just beyond the glass and wood of the shuttered windows Tom wove a tale worthy of Penelope's guile, grasping bits from images hidden far away even from his own mind.

The visions Tom formed of gentle powdery snow kisses steered clear of any notion that Boston in winter could create its own horrifying scenes, but Tom had a willing audience of believers who had likely never known true winter. At Robert's half-concealed smile, Tom was aware that his memory held images of a harsher season than Tom's depiction, but he knew Tom's intent, so silently conceded and everyone's fears subsided for a bit as they envisioned lovely scenes of mild, postcard winters filled with games and adventures of gliding on a cushion of snow and ice.

After feeding the children from the ample larder Tom and Robert had carried upstairs, everyone seemed able to relax somewhat and accept they would still have hours to wait before the storm's passage. Companionable groups formed in the spacious hall as Warren Miller rocked his baby daughter Sophie to sleep with a fiercely focused attention to his precious task. Warren's son Charlie and the young Laraby boys played quietly near the boys' now-calmer mother. Mary Ellen and Sarah helped form a protected area screened from the others for Bridget to nurse her infant. Robert and Sheryl Miller spoke calmly with the elderly neighbors, Mrs. Hoglen and Mrs. Kelsey, whom Lottie had convinced to join the picnickers for a "short visit." Meanwhile, Tom inched my chair closer to Lottie's seat on a small bench.

"Thank you, Tom," she said as Tom approached.

"For what?" Tom asked simply.

She looked surprised but smiled, "For being here mostly, I suppose. For working like a Trojan to encase us here safely during this beastly storm. And possibly the most important reason is for making a Boston winter seem like playing in the clouds—I won't ever forget that picture. I've not seen winter in New England, but I imagine there's a bit more to it than gentle, flakey kisses. The children were mesmerized. I hadn't realized you had such a gift for storytelling."

Her hand-over-fist compliments had Tom blushing such that he whispered thanks to Heaven for the dim lighting. He mumbled, "I blame you entirely, I'm afraid. I haven't a poetic bone in my wanderer's soul, Lottie, but I knew you needed me, so it just came out somehow. I'm certainly glad I'm a reader, that's all."

Lottie smiled so beautifully, Tom could hardly think. She looked toward Robert, and unnecessarily lowered her voice even more, saying, "Thank you, too, for understanding that what I needed to help Robert and Bridget was just your agreement even though you didn't know the situation. That wasn't very kind of me; I just couldn't have Robert sending his niece and the baby out again over some silly sense of pride or embarrassment. Bridget isn't married; her…the man who is Suzanne's father left the island as soon as Bridget told him she was expecting a child, poor thing. She's a good girl, and was crushed to find out this terrible man didn't really love her. It broke Robert's heart really."

Tom was listening so intently, Lottie stopped abruptly and said, "What? I'm rambling, aren't I?"

"No," he assured her. "I was just thinking how incredibly generous and sincere you are; many people in your position would have put them both out, but you treat all of them as if they're family."

With this volley, now she was blushing, and Tom could have played this game and watched her lovely blooming face for hours had their mutual reverie not been instantly shattered with the sound of breaking glass downstairs.

Charlie squealed in surprise. All calming thoughts of romping through fluffy clouds exploded in a flash as the adults realized the fury of the storm had intensified while the children sensed the tension. Having known this might occur eventually, Robert and Tom had planned to move the group into a more protected area if necessary. The men had blocked the windows of Lottie's bed chamber with wood on the inside as well as the shutters on the outside, but that made the room more cramped than the hallway and much darker.

Without coordinating words, Lottie stepped up to gather the children to move to her room and light more lamps while Robert, Warren, and Tom took up lanterns to inspect the damage they knew they would discover somewhere on the floors below. The men left to the soothing words Lottie addressed to the three frightened boys, "I have many more books for you to read in my room, and we can build a huge tent if we open up the armoire. My brother Patrick and I used to do it all the time...."

The breakage was minimal—a glass section had taken the brunt of the wind-buffeted shutter—but the evidence proved the incredible intensity of the wind. That the shutters, designed for the express purpose of protecting the fragile glass, could have indirectly caused this breakage reminded them all how firmly the powerful storm held everyone in its unyielding force. This tiny cluster of friends was at the mercy of a tyrant that could easily break through their meager defenses at any moment to render them exposed, helpless, and utterly destroyed. Tom felt extremely vulnerable at that moment. They all could only guess how long their torturous waiting may last in this present state of limbo.

Robert's words echoed Tom's confused thoughts, "I imagine we must wait until morning, Sir, to discover how much more damage we shall find."

"Yes," Tom replied absently. Before the storm, Tom had helped Robert stuff old rags into the gaping glass that likely had been weak because the other panes held, but they dared not open the window shutters or any doors to peer into the storm. The frames rattled as the wind buffeted the house already. The sheets of rain seemed to have fallen back into a kneeling position. And the house-shaking, terrific wind danced around the building and whirled off in another direction when the disturbing noises outside seemed more distant, then all of a sudden, the shriek would rise up again, sounding very close, and then would slam into a different part of the structure.

Warren left Robert and Tom to reassure the others, and Robert opened his mouth as if to speak but closed it again undecided. As Tom knew this might be their only chance to speak privately without eliciting attention and concern, Tom encouraged Robert to speak. "Robert, did you want to say anything?"

"Thank you, Sir," Robert sighed as he spoke. "I realize I have no true right to say this as a servant, but the Gallaghers have always treated me more kindly than I deserve." He paused as if steeling himself to say something unpleasant. Tom couldn't be sure the direction Robert would go, so he remained silent as Robert thought through his comments.

Tom was relieved and touched when Robert rushed on saying, "Well, Sir. I feel privileged to be assisting you this way. You have been quite resourceful and calm in the light of what I can now see is much more of a dangerous emergency than I expected initially. Mr. Daniel will be heartily pleased and grateful to learn of the full extent of your courage in protecting Cashlin. And Miss Charlotte, of course."

"Thank you, Robert," Tom said and smiled. Tom was struck by Robert's kind albeit unexpected sentiments in part because he'd never heard the reticent butler speak so much at any one time. And because his position of needing to know everything happening around him while presenting an attitude of discrete ignorance made Robert somewhat daunting. He had previously seemed a bit unreal, but now Tom could see Robert as much more human. Inwardly, Tom praised God for giving Robert the strength and wisdom to speak those words of encouragement. Tom sensed in that moment he would need all the support he could muster.

As they mounted the stairs together, Robert added in a tone of nervous camaraderie and extraordinary license granted to him only by the raging storm that had grasped their attention so tightly, "I do hope, Sir, that I am able to offer my very best wishes to you and our mistress very soon as well. Nothing would give me more pleasure."

Laughing out loud at how thin his disguise of concerned acquaintance must appear to Robert, Tom graciously thanked him, adding, "We've not exactly made any pronouncements regarding my incredible joy—Mary Ellen would likely flay me alive were I to cut any courtship corners—perhaps we should deal with one storm at a time."

"Exactly so, Sir," Robert declared again in his most professionally detached voice. And but for the ill-lit passageway, Tom would have sworn he saw the glimmer of Robert's teeth in a knowing smile.

When the men returned, Lottie was reading Peter Rabbit to the boys who were showing signs of weary resignation despite the still early hour. Tom's watch showed only minutes past six in the evening, but sleep would help them ignore their fears of the wind and rain.

Mary Ellen was crooning "Tura Lura Lura" to Bridget's baby who seemed enchantingly oblivious to any imminent danger. She was content to be passed between the women who took turns adoring her baby-ness.

The room was crowded with all the anxious bodies waiting out the storm unsure of what they were actually waiting to happen, and yet, oddly, Tom felt a comfortable sense of privacy as if the others intuited Lottie and Tom had life-altering plans to discuss. As the rest slept or read or chatted, the couple sat seemingly alone in a world they were learning together how best to color and flavor and imagine.

Lottie smiled as she swept a protective glance at what she still deemed her guests and said, "I do recall telling you we surely would have a chance to continue our interrupted discussion from yesterday. These wild tempests do tire me, but I can never manage to sleep, so perhaps we could talk now."

The storm wasn't as violent at this moment in the night as it had been only hours before, but the wind was still too strong for comfort. The rain alternated between angry staccato jabs at the shutters pelting down an erratic beat that could not quite realize the grandeur of music and a teasing spray misting the walls as if a gentle reminder of purification. Rarely did the shower stay calm long enough to lull the waiting inhabitants into an easy mindset, and the storm played on feverishly regardless. Even with this two-toned water dance, the listeners were aware that it never stopped completely.

"I wonder," Tom said as he looked at Lottie, bringing his storm-wary mind back from the water's manipulation on his senses, "if I'll ever be able to hear rain and not think of us and our beginning. It was raining yesterday when we talked, too."

Lottie raised the corners of her mouth into a comfortable smile, but said nothing, so Tom continued, "I don't mean I think God sent down a devastating storm just so we could have the cover of a storm in which to spend time together alone." He looked at the other occupants of the makeshift shelter as Lottie raised an eyebrow and smiled even more brightly. "Well, *almost* alone," Tom corrected. "But it is as if the Heavens are heralding a creation so new and beautiful it needed a phenomenal stage setting: *Look out world—pay attention now! This is important.*" Tom smiled at this image.

"I like to think of it that way," she replied, "but I'm fairly certain two rather intelligent young people such as we seem to be likely would have come up with something even without all this dramatic divine assistance."

"True," Tom smiled.

"Your version is far more poetic though," she said softly and then more seriously continued, "Tell me what you've been thinking about, Tom."

"You," Tom answered truthfully. She *was* all he had been thinking about for weeks now.

"Stop it," she looked down fighting a smile. "You know what I mean. If we're...together," she blushed so beautifully at the word, "then you can't be a priest. Are you absolutely certain about that? I feel responsible for derailing such a long-held intention— even though I don't want to apologize."

"No," Tom said slowly. "No apologies. No regrets. Liam and I have talked about my vocation quite a bit since I came to Galveston. Even well before you came into such focus for me. And I realize no one beyond the two of you will ever believe me when I say that my love for you is not the reason I will *not* become a priest."

Lottie nodded encouragement to Tom and sat with her attention riveted on his face. Tom continued to put into words thoughts he was only now able to articulate. "I suppose we shouldn't blame anyone too harshly for jumping to that conclusion; it appears as such on the surface. But I can see so clearly now what I have known for a long time—long before I met you—that God's plan for me did not include the priesthood."

"What made you know that?" she asked quietly.

"Well," Rom started, "before my Uncle Tim just about forced my parents to allow me this time away to reflect, I'd never even allowed myself to formulate questions about what I wanted. My mother had already determined my course. I do sense she did it in love—or her version of love anyway. It was her passion and highest wish, and I accepted that to be my desire as well."

"But it wasn't?" Lottie asked as if hoping to glean every morsel of meaning from this intricate puzzle that was an integral part of them now.

"Yes and no," Tom replied, still grappling with this recent revelation himself and determining how best to introduce it to her. "I didn't know it wasn't what I wanted. Does that make sense?"

She nodded so Tom continued. "I wanted to serve God and obeying my mother seemed like a good place to start, I guess. So I willingly went along. Ever since I was little. But part of me—I don't know—my heart? My mind? Part of me hung back feeling something didn't fit together. I figured I'd learn someday how to make it fit. Or that it would automatically work out somehow."

"Did you ever tell you mother about that feeling or your uncle? Is that why he insisted on your delay?" she asked.

"I'm not sure why Uncle Tim did what he did. Or why my mother was so adamant; they were both so intense that night Tim brought all this up. But I never spoke these kinds of words to anyone until Liam and I talked about the existence of random acts."

"Random acts?" Lottie asked looking confused, which puckered her brow with a delightful crease Tom hadn't seen before. Almost like a linear and vertical dimple but on her forehead.

"You know," Tom began watching for the line he'd caused to disappear as her facial muscles relaxed—what a beautiful face she had! "Whether God allows things to just happen or if everything that happens to us has a set purpose. That kind of thing."

"What did you two learned scholars decide on that point?" Again her expressive face had Tom charmed as if he were some instinct-driven serpent beckoned from his basket. Her eyes flashed amusement that also twitched her lips at the corners while her marble-smooth brow was the bastion of sincere contemplation and discernment. Tom's intoxicated mind surrendered to the play of her features until her voice pulled him out of this reverie, recognizing she'd repeated the question he hadn't heard distinctly the first time either. Tom caught the inquisitive lilt at the end of her words but had no other clues.

"Forgive me," he begged, "I'm guilty of staring and blatant adoration. If you'll ask me once more, I promise I'll attend." Tom even hazarded a touch the first time; he deliberately felt her supple skin, lightly fingering her wrist. Tom would never embarrass Lottie by some showy outward display of affection, but that she never flinched or rejected his touch made the subtle brushing of skin every bit more intimate than had she been uncomfortable with his closeness. His touch and her accepting response made her so real. And ironically, this quiet reality was the stuff of his dreams.

She laughed playfully, shifting slightly to expose the inside of her wrist so Tom could more easily explore her beautiful palm and asked, "What exactly did you see just now in your staring, Mr. McDermott?"

"Was that your first question? Or is this an addendum to the first, once removed?" Tom asked. "I fear you'll only befuddle an already very...well, fuddled mind, my dear, dear Miss Gallagher if you continue to interject inquiry after inquiry with no time for response."

"Ah quite so," Lottie played along, gently pressing Tom's exploring hand now enclosed over hers. "I do digress. My first question repeated for the benefit of those with wandering imaginations, was what you and the esteemed and learned Father Liam decided about...how should I say? Random...randomitity. My second—do tell, can you process two inquiries at once? Excellent. My second was what did you see as you stared off so far afield you could not even hear my voice mere inches away?"

"I see. Yes," Tom meticulously measured his rough hand against her tiny beautiful palm by flexing his curious fingers repeatedly beside hers. "Well, first things first—what I saw was a lovely peek into my future. Oh drat it all, Miss Gallagher—that first responds to the second question, doesn't it? Ahhh…. Permission respectively requested to answer the random questions randomly?"

"Granted," she chimed with the delightful mixture of seriousness and winsome play that marks children of all ages. Her fingers lightly danced on Tom's palm as he continued to explore this incredible sensory landscape he had so recently discovered.

"Actually, as with so many of our lofty, nocturnal philosophical debates, I don't think we ever did come to any straight answer that night," Tom said sounding far more somber than he'd intended. "We both acknowledged that our God does have absolute control. He does have a set purpose for us, and bringing me to Galveston was no mistake. So, I think 'random' lost the debate."

Lottie's soft eyes now reflected Tom's more serious but no less ardent voice. She smiled and whispered, "I'm so glad."

Tom continued as they sat, surrounded by a dozen people, but totally alone in a brand new world of their own design, "Lottie, I love you with a passion I barely understand even now. It changes everything, but not because anything is doubtful in my mind about us, only because everything I've ever done or been in my life up to this juncture led to me being able to see you as the blessing you are, and know I will praise God daily for allowing me to serve Him with you by my side. And help you serve Him." Tom felt Lottie's beautiful hand tremble in his own.

He continued defining his new-found philosophy. "This focus is my reality—no artist other than the Creator of the universe could have coordinated so many distinct lives, so many disparate emotions to bring us here on the threshold of a future so bright it could only be divinely created. I have never even thought of any other woman. Not just because of my mother's priesthood plans for me, but because, for me, there is no other, and could never have been anyone else. I so clearly see that now, Lottie. You are my soul's mate and always have been—waiting here for me. I want us to spend the rest of our lives together, and then I'll play with you and our babies in Heaven. This isn't the time or the place, because I want to do everything properly, as you deserve, but I will very soon speak to your father to ascertain his blessing so we can marry as soon as you deem proper. I will defer to your wisdom on all points of etiquette, darling, dearest Lottie, if you will kindly keep in mind I would stand today on your very hearth if my public protestations of devotion would be an acceptable bond for us. Unofficially, just for us, tell me, darling, will you marry me?"

The silent tears trickling down Lottie's nodding face touched Tom's overwhelmed heart, and they sat silently relishing this outpouring of their like emotions.

Lottie smiled at Tom and spoke in a whisper, "I will my own darling Tom. Could you even wonder?"

As Tom beamed back at her in a glow of light and joy as they huddled against the raging storm outside, she continued, "I want to talk more with you and dear, dear Liam about how deft and sure God is in creating our blessings. Just think of all the miniscule choices and chances that happened in both our lives to bring us here today together. I could so easily have gone with Father on his trip or been away visiting. But, of course, God knew better. This is where I belong...forever."

"I'm so, so happy," Tom gushed, thinking it rather urbane even as he mumbled the words. "I must respectfully request, however, my dear Miss Gallagher," he slipped back into playful mode to ease them back from the edge of tension, albeit such a beautiful intensity, their discussion had taken them.

"Yes, Mr. McDermott?" she picked up the banter.

"You simply must limit your invite list," he frowned slightly.

She smiled with understanding glancing around.

"I simply wish to have you to myself," Tom faltered, wavering on the brink of too intense again. "Funny how I can wish to kiss you so terribly much when I have never experienced that specific blessing in my life."

Lottie blushed in exquisite shades contemplating Tom's desire.

Again the near silence was rent by a terrifying noise from some indistinct quarter beyond our walls, jarring all into heightened anxiety. Their bubbled solitude instantly crackled into exquisite shards each a brilliant crystal as they both actively drew the others closer with soothing words and the camaraderie of proximity.

Robert was the first to speak after the crash they all tried silently to identify, knowing they could never forget it. He said, "We're so fortunate Miss Lottie, to be inside dry and warm. May I bring you anything? You haven't eaten this evening."

One of the babies began to whimper caught between an inexplicable fear and interrupted slumber. All eyes moved from the blocked window and the horrific noise to the calm man who seemed to have asked such an incongruent question as if this were a normal day, and he were going about his duties.

Lottie began to shake her head to refuse still trembling from the fright when she realized the wise older man's words had nothing to do with food. He was a trained ally with her, and took the lead when she faltered.

"Yes...yes, Robert," Standing, Lottie said, trying to disguise any tremor in her voice. "I think we all could do with a bite from Sarah's delicious store. Mattie, would you enjoy a cookie, Sweet Angel? And Mary Ellen, I must insist that I have a turn with Susie. She'd be a grown woman before anyone else could hold her if it were up to you!"

The ensuing bustle helped them all as they stretched and moved out of the fear-induced lethargy. The group had been hours in this safe but artificial environment waiting for reality to return. They could only wonder at what destruction resulted from the resounding crash. For now they were safe and blind to images they would not have believed possible had they been forced to witness the destruction as it occurred all around outside and could only have served to terrify them.

As the inhabitants settled again into an anxious waiting, they again heard a deafening crash. This one was closer and both Bridget and Mary Ellen screamed before clasping hands over horrified mouths.

"Tom!" Lottie called out and looked across the room to where he stood. Tom was at her side in a moment and felt more than knew that she realized the house had been struck by something this time.

"Robert and I will go check," he replied to her unspoken request.

Warren Miller was calming his wife and children, but called over, "I'll go, too, Tom."

Tom nodded to both men as they hurriedly took up lamps to investigate they knew not what. Down the massive stairs, the wind howling outside sounded so much louder than in Lottie's back room, Tom instantly prayed out loud, "Oh, Father protect us all."

Warren involuntarily responded, "Amen" as he clapped a reassuring hand on Tom's shoulder.

What sounded like a tree branch striking the bricks of the porch that surrounded almost the entire second floor ended up being a large door that had evidence of having been ripped violently from its hinges. The solid rectangle had wedged into an alcove on the porch between the low brick wall that served as the railing to the porch and a wall of the house. The wind battered it repeatedly against the bricks.

Somewhat protected from the still strong wind, the men were quickly able to dislodge the door and carry it inside the large ballroom on that floor so it would cause no more damage.

"I wonder where that door came from," Warren mused aloud as they began re-securing the shutters, but finished in amazement, "Oh my God in Heaven!"

Robert and Tom looked up in time to see a surge of brownish water coming up the side street only a few hundred feet from where they stood on the covered porch. Momentarily contained within the narrow channel formed by the feeble fences abutting each side, the wave pressed its way down the alley. As if appearing out of nowhere, water gushed into every opening, carrying along with it debris they could barely recognize in the blinding mist and disorienting wind of the night's eerie dimness. It was rising rapidly and covered part of the yard and street below. They had no idea what havoc the storm had wrecked beyond the blocked windows of their fortress.

Robert yelled over the pounding chaos, "The waves have flooded up from the beach; this isn't merely a rain overflow—those wooden houses will surely be destroyed! We must get back inside."

Transfixed into an awed paralysis, Tom only moved at the electric touch on his arm as Lottie instantly materialized beside him. Tom hadn't noticed her entrance and didn't know how long she'd stood by him. She had to shout to be heard only inches away, "Tom, can the water get to us here?"

Robert answered as Tom seemed unable to move or think or speak, "Miss Lottie, Cashlin has never flooded. We will be safe." They all sighed collectively never doubting if Robert knew this for certain or just had a knack for encouragement in the midst of disaster.

Jerking his head up, Tom awoke as if from a fitful sleep ready to move them all back to the quiet sanctum above this teeming cauldron when they all saw it at once. Lottie's hand closed tightly on Tom's arm, her scream inaudible yet horrifying. Warren was visibly shaken, and Tom feared Robert would fall to his knees.

A makeshift raft—was it the top of a table? The side of a building?—was pulsing into sight near enough to their vantage on the second floor to see a tall man drenched and shirtless clinging to the edges of the rectangle lying on top of a small woman and two terrified children to pin them to this life preserver. As if caught in some immovable trance, the Cashlin group watched the small raft in horror and thought they would continue to flow beyond view, but Robert realized before the others the raft would collide with the ornamental gazebo on the far side of the estate. He yelled as it become the reality he'd projected. Suspended in what seemed like mid-air, the raft caught tenuously on the metal scroll work lattice of the gazebo jerking the clinging group's life preserver forcefully but stopping its violent floating progress.

Lottie screamed, "We have to get to them somehow! Robert. Thomas, please! Those poor children. Please!"

Robert and Tom looked at each other and saw only terror reflected back. Tom tried to formulate a plan to somehow drag the raft from its perilous perch knowing reasonable timing and rational thought were useless. "We need rope, Robert," Tom called to him as he began taking off shoes and his coat, knowing these would weigh him down in the water. "I'll wade and swim to the raft and take a rope we can secure to this column."

"Mr. Tom," Robert seemed at a loss, "All my rope is in the shed on the other side of the grounds— likely underwater by now."

"What are we going to do?" Warren cried. "We can't just leave them there. No telling how long that raft will hold them if we get another wave. It's a miracle they made it from wherever they started." He too was stripping off cumbersome layers on the brick porch.

They turned in our indecision at the clattering sound of another crash but from inside the mansion this time. Lottie was scrambling through the massive folds of burgundy material from the plush draperies she'd just ripped down from the ceilings high windows. "Here," she yelled in a fury of concentration. "Take these cords first, and Robert and I can tie together the curtains themselves. Hurry! Go now."

Robert, Warren, and Tom instantly ran to help her disentangle the stout curtain cords, tying one end to the outside column. Warren and Tom didn't wait to double check if the ropes were secure, but dashed with one end each working themselves over the edge of the porch and navigating down to the ground with whatever footholds came to their aid, into the wind and rain with only one goal in mind.

Robert stayed with Lottie, who tore through the material in her lap with no regard to the expense or ruin of the once opulent curtains. She willed herself to remain focused and calm as she transformed these now superfluous decorations into her new purpose.

18.   Prayers

Therefore I tell you, whatever you ask for in prayer, believe that you have received it, and it will be yours. Mark 11:24

Liam faced the same terrors the mixed group at Cashlin did, but with fewer friends to bolster his spirits in the face of unprecedented fears. Prayers had always carried Liam through trying times. He liked to pray and supposed most people saw prayer like that—a life preserver of sorts to cling to when the waves threaten to topple their boats. Liam admitted later to worrying instead of ignoring all anxiety through prayer as others may have expected him to have done during the storm.

The storm was setting in fiercely as Liam, Sean, and Father O'Mallary returned from securing the church to the relatively safe haven of the old rectory. Sean calmed immediately, but Father O'Mallary could barely stop fidgeting enough to sit still. He became increasingly upset and refused to adhere to any set plan of action the others could devise for mere moments before moving in a different direction.

Liam's first project was to settle the older gentlemen together in his upstairs study as the safest interior room away from the usual brunt of wind and rain from these types of storms. Sean collected Father O'Mallary's Bible and his worn violin, the only two material possessions that could calm him if he were to be consoled at all. Liam silently applauded the old serving man's attempt to soothe his master.

Clicking off the list in his mind, Liam knew the three men had plenty of food in the house for the day or two they may have to serve themselves in the aftermath of the storm. The most inconvenient parts of a storm always come afterward, Liam thought as he catalogued all he would be tasked with in the days following. Some parishioners always suffered more damages than others. They would seek solace and even shelter at St. Patrick's, which was only right.

Breaking Liam's concentration, Father O'Mallary scraped his chair against the floor. He would have none of Sean's attempts to settle the old man down for patient waiting.

"Why on Earth would I play that thing at a time like this, man?" Father O'Mallary barked at the unblinking Sean as he glared at the old violin.

The usual half-mumbled apology was not forthcoming, which surprised Liam, but seemed not to phase Sean. The two older men had been together much longer than the time Liam had been on the scene. Best to leave them to their own devices. Somehow, the three settled into an uneasy routine.

They all paced. They sighed heavily in turn. They continued to check the window periodically as if their meticulous positioning of the curtain would change the atmospheric conditions raging outside. Even as this incongruity crossed Liam's mind repeatedly, he couldn't stop his actions.

Finally, Father O'Mallary did tire of walking the room's perimeter and ignoring the noises they could ill disguise. He turned abruptly and announced, "I will be in my own room, Liam. This flood will not lessen by my feeble attempts to control it. We should all attempt to sleep."

Liam didn't sleep that night, but feeling a bit guilty, was glad for the quiet the garrulous old priest's departure afforded the room. In this favorite of rooms, Liam was affably silent with Sean, who was obviously basking in the delight of an unexpected time for reading in a parlor far better equipped to facilitate that pleasure than his own attic room.

The wind shook the building so severely, Liam feared he'd chosen unwisely in not seeking the more solid structure of the stone church. But it was too late to move now and one felt safer at home in times like these, he thought. After that first fretful hour, he'd put off pacing. He couldn't see anything outside the window anyway with the shutters Sean had reattached during a brief calm. He had left these unfastened at first so they could watch, but both agreed after the first rages of the storm slackened for a few minutes that they should secure them as tightly as they could despite the loss of the view to what was happening beyond the meager panes of glass. The old exterior shutters were flimsy at best—more ornamental than functional, but Sean fastened each side regardless. Then once back inside, they secured the inner shutters as well—these were more like small doors that folded in on themselves to wear an everyday face of aesthetic propriety. Rarely in use, the stout panels seemed out of place and awkward, intruding themselves into the room and shrinking the comfortable area by blocking the light and air.

This work completed in a flutter of active purpose, they fell again into the ease of quiet waiting. Liam created lists to pass the time—supplies that would most be needed by the parishioners, families most able to offer financial assistance to those unable to provide for themselves, and regular events to be postponed a week or two. Storms seemed to bring out a generous side of people by slightly disrupting routines and schedules, Liam mused.

19.   Rescue

The Lord will rescue me from every evil attack and will bring me safely to his heavenly kingdom. 2 Timothy 4:18

As if in an instant, the storm and the Cashlin group part in it had changed drastically and entirely. They were no longer a lucky cohort of safe, dry observers quietly awaiting the end of what seemed to them to be a mildly serious, somewhat inconvenient natural event. With no time for deliberation or conscious acceptance, they became determined participants in the history of this moment, warring against the strongest forces of nature, risking life and future stability with a desperate attempt to save these strangers who otherwise would certainly perish. This is the stuff of legend, although Tom and the others didn't realize it at the time. The only significance was the now. Not one of them questioned their actions; no mind paused to calculate the costs and risks. They could no more have ignored this silent call for help than they could have stopped breathing. They simply thrust themselves forward, leaving analysis and reflection for later, more quiet times.

As Warren and Tom groped their way through the punishing wind with glass-sharp rain pricking their faces and arms, Lottie and Robert continued to fashion long ropes from the stout draperies. Lottie paused only long enough to run back upstairs to inform the others and bring Mary Ellen, Sarah, and Sheryl down to help. Mrs. Laraby, realizing only now the severity of the situation and fervently praying for her absent husband, volunteered to stay and help Bridget soothe the babies and the elderly neighbors. It was Mrs. Laraby who had the maternal intuition to calm Mrs. Hoglen and Mrs. Kelsey both by asking them to rock the infants.

This well-placed distribution of duties brought to light the little-understood element of human nature that longs to serve and be of use, not only in tragic situations but perhaps even more poignantly throughout the mundane movements of life. Mrs. Laraby would have been most surprised of all had an expert told her how well she had addressed this primitive psychological need for the two elderly women she nurtured; she only knew in an instant that they needed something to occupy their worried minds, and the children needed to be loved.

The others collected whatever they could think of to comfort the stranded foursome with no doubt even entertained that the planned rescue mission might fall short of success. Lottie glowed with determined confidence and had even shed her initial sense of terrorized anxiety when she first realized the predicament this stranded family on the floating debris faced. She now only busied herself and encouraged the others with what the newcomers would need to become part of the enclave.

Warren reached the gazebo before Tom did, and the woman on the raft was the first to comprehend that her family may indeed have saviors. She shouted to the man who held her on the now stationary platform. When Tom climbed up the other end of the metal structure dragging the rope, the man smiled feebly and for the first time in his life Tom understood what gratitude really meant. From the terror of facing certain death to the reality of assisting their rescuers in the still perilous task of getting their family to a stable shelter, the couple reacted swiftly but with the buoy of a renewed hope that relaxed their weary muscles and calmed their frayed nerves. Screaming over the incessant howl of the wind and gesturing their intentions the best they could, the adults were able to communicate enough to reassure the children they were safe—almost. The group still had to traverse the lawns again through the rain and wind and rising waters, but compared to the ordeal this bedraggled family had endured to arrive at this juncture, the trek across the yard tied to each other with the cord from Lottie's draperies was far less daunting.

With faith and trust born of necessity, the parents surrendered their children, one each to Warren and to Tom. The men quickly climbed down the lattice and decided to have Warren take both children back to the porch where the others waited to bring the children inside. Tom scrambled back up the makeshift ladder, and the man and Tom secured the woman to Tom. They started to descend. Only two steps down the structure though, Tom stopped and motioned to the man to come down with them; Tom decided in an instant they could secure the man o them.

Tom had have never been more convinced in his life that God sends actual legions of angels to help in the most desperate times than in those few seconds, for just as the adults stepped off the lattice onto the ground, a tremendous gust of wind lifted up the table top now unburdened of its weight that had served as the family's raft, and the force of the wind sheared off the ornamental iron dome of the gazebo as well. Paralyzed and utterly in awe, Tom and his charges craned their necks to watch the now suspended objects that looked so incongruent with no support holding them aloft. Three frightened children searching for the warmth of reassuring parental arms; they brought their shocked stares back to the immediate danger.

They couldn't even imagine how the harsh wind could become stronger, but it seemed it was attempting that impossibility just out of spite. The howling wind sounds became piercing squeals that fell into mournful, guttural moans and worked back up again to shrieking echoes. The three strangers uttered silent prayers of thanksgiving as they ran and stumbled toward the house with the woman half carried, half dragged between the man and Tom.

Lottie was waiting for us just under the canopy of the porch with towels and blankets. Relieved and beside herself with the joy of their now secure outcome, she busied herself with the rescued woman who seemed to be waking to the actual situation at hand. As one deep in concentration, the drenched woman had been relatively quiet as they transferred the children off the raft and then again during her own race to the security of the house. Now inside and out of immediate danger, the woman began sobbing and speaking incoherently, rocking back and forth and hugging Lottie to her as if still in the perilous wind. Lottie tried to soothe her but could not make sense of her words. The man looked just as animated but paced by the edge of the porch, seeming to contemplate returning to the storm to retrieve some valuable item on the raft, now swept away in the flood.

Tom looked over the head of the woman and into Lottie's concerned eyes, trying to ascertain what they could do to alleviate their fears. Perhaps the woman was anxious because she couldn't see her two children whom Mary Ellen had taken upstairs to dry and clothe.

Tom tried this assumption first, "Ma'am, your children are fine. We're just finding them something dry to wear. We can go see them immediately."

Lottie picked up Tom's attempt when this assurance didn't seem to calm the distraught woman. Gently stroking the woman's wet hair, Lottie crooned as to a sick child, "Sweetheart, let's get you into something warm as well, and then you can all eat something. You're safe now. You don't have to worry. The children are fine. The storm will pass soon."

The woman blinked up into Lottie's eyes in the confused manner of a feverish child and seemed to comprehend, but then said very clearly, "My babies. I must go find my babies. They'll be so frightened."

Lottie sighed with relief as she crooned, "Ah then. No, they're fine, dear. Your babies are upstairs with Mary Ellen. Let's go see them now, and you'll see. Your babies are here with you and safe. You just need to be able to see them, don't you?"

"No, no," the woman insisted in a moaning voice trying to stand and disentangle herself from Lottie, poised for escape. Her wet garments clung to her straining body and made her petite frame seem even slighter.

Abruptly and with a definite air of resolve, the man stopped pacing and stepped up to the woman, speaking quickly but deliberately as he placed his gangly hands on her heaving shoulders, "Joan. Listen to me, Joan. I'll go and find them, but you must promise me you'll stay here with Katie and Michael. Promise?" Their eyes locked, connected in some far-off struggle only they could fathom.

She stared at him, willing her strained nerves to understand, and nodded, but could only mutter again, falling back down into Lottie's arms and onto the floor, "My babies. Please. My babies. Oh, God, please!"

The others were paralyzed watching this exchange. Caring fervently, but grasping none of the moment's import, they stared and waited. Then it dawned on Tom; the children upstairs were not all of her children. Lord have mercy. They had been separated in the flood waters. Of course. It was miraculous the rescued four had been able to stay afloat on the temporary raft. How could children have resisted the brutal wind they had seen and felt? What were the chances of the other children surviving this? Had the family been all together and these fallen off in the turbulent waters? How old were the others? How many children were there? How could they ever find them now? No one should be out in this wind and rain. From minute to minute, the ferocity of the storm changed and intensified. No one was safe in this merciless gale unless inside a fortress-like structure such as the Cashlin group had, but how could you not go search for your own children? Even if they were surely dead.

Lottie held the woman closer as she, too, realized the horrific truth of what the few words between the two must mean. Tom could see the pained understanding in her beautiful, loving eyes. This couple would never be strangers now; the small band of strangers were living through their tragedy with them. It was now everyone's tragedy.

Taking gentle control in a way she does so wonderfully, Lottie turned to this traumatized woman and spoke quietly but insisted, "Joan, we're going upstairs now to get away from this window. We'll leave the men to plan the rescue, but Katie and Michael need you now. They'll be worried, and they need their mother. Come on; up we go. We'll get you some dry clothes, too. You and I are about the same size, I suspect." Continuing her soothing banter, Lottie said, "Sheryl, dear, please come help us, won't you?"

Lottie glanced up at Tom with such concern and love in her eyes that he knew she realized the improbability of any end to this encounter other than death and loss and grief, but with a look that also showed her staunch faith in miracles. She trusted Tom could somehow orchestrate this miracle, too. The couple seemed to have lived a lifetime in this one momentous day they'd originally planned to spend picnicking as a diversion to their private meeting. Had it been only yesterday they had huddled in the rain-streaked doorway of St. Patrick's?

As the women filed out of the disheveled room, Warren and Tom drew the woman's husband back into the shelter of the room to determine how best to proceed. Tom was afraid he was in shock initially, but he looked with comprehending eyes as Tom repeated his question, "Your wife is evidently concerned for your other children?"

"Yes," the weary man answered, then shook his head. "No. I mean, yes, there *are* two more children. There's Katie…no, Katie's here; she's safe. It's little Laura I have to go get. I'm Paul Bruce. And Brian; Brian isn't here either; he'll be fine; he had Laura with him on the stairs; I saw them together, and then....That's Joan Coverdale." He looked up, concerned he wasn't getting the facts straight in his narrative. After a moment, he began again, "We're not married. Yet. We will be soon. The water...it...it just....The children never had a chance to grab our raft. We barely took hold of it as it lurched by the flooded porch. The water kept...I thought they were there....Everything happened so quickly. First, we saw, no....One minute...." Stopping again, he turned to accept the shirt Robert had silently left to procure for him from the depths of some closet in another region of the enormous house. Paul never picked up his rambling thought; their minds were all so disturbed, no one noticed.

Of course, Tom realized. Tom had thought the woman was familiar, but in the chaos had not connected her distraught face with that of the pleasant owner of the bakery near the shore. Father Liam was a regular there, and Tom had been there with him several times. She attended St. Patrick's as well as the man standing here with him; Tom recognized them all now. The children were always polite and quiet; clean if not overly well dressed. Four tow-headed children who now knew what Hell looked like. So many questions to ask, but none so important now as what to do about finding the children they all knew were likely lost in this devastation without adding their own tragic deaths to the misery this family would suffer when the wind finally calmed down.

Robert spoke from the window to which he had retreated in his unobtrusive, habitual tidying that marked his waking hours. Always orderly, always catering to needs others wouldn't even consider significant, Robert had run Cashlin efficiently for decades. Now he set about ordering this chaos.

He was coiling the rope the men had dropped on the porch after our mad dashes across the lawn. "I believe," Robert began, "we should re-secure these shutters, Sir." Before any of us could look up from our personal reveries, Robert had gasped calling out loudly, "Oh my God! It *is* a miracle. Sirs, come quickly. Hurry to them." The older man, uncharacteristically animated, pointed to the far side of the lawns where the waters were stopped by a length of stone garden fencing.

The others lunged to the slick porch to see Robert's miracle. Two forms were clinging to the edge of the stone wall, plastered there by the wind. Robert acted first by taking the curtain cords again and securing one end to the stout columns. Warren and Tom repeated their previous actions, joined now by Paul, praying they would reach the wall in time. Through the blurring rain, the men could not determine if these new castaways were the children they'd prayed for only moments before or two other unfortunates who equally needed their lifelines, but they raced toward them with a renewed energy. Paul was the first to reach the wall and put a restraining hand on each of the small bodies limp with exhaustion. As Tom arrived behind him ready to hoist the forms over the wall, Tom witnessed the beautiful recognition in the children's faces as they smiled into Paul's eyes wet with tears and rain. That fleeting moment will live with Tom forever as image of faith and love and hope. Warren was already adroitly looping ends of the strong rope over the shoulders and under the arms of each child.

In the lashing rain, they didn't stop to contemplate the phenomenal odds of this reunion; they praised God through their redoubled strength to maneuver all five bodies back to the security of the house. This meddling group wind was angrier now, cheated out of more victims. We would be allowed no more free forays into the storm for now. The branches of one of the large trees cracked and began swaying dangerously close to them as they crawled the last few yards to the house, and Tom agreed with Robert that they must close the windows and shutters and return to the more secure location deeper inside. How many other struggling victims might still come by this portal?

They couldn't risk compromising the safety of our huddled group upstairs, they knew, but all of them ached to think someone may need help, and they wouldn't be able to reach them.

Warren carried the dripping, little girl and Paul hoisted the young boy over his shoulder as they climbed through the tall windows into the room and through to the wide staircase where Lottie was helping Joan come down when they heard the men calling to them triumphantly. It was the first sound of joy to come into the fear-filled halls since the darkening sky had driven the festivities inside. In the middle of the first wide landing, the mother greedily reached for her two missing children and held them to her heart with the other children beaming behind her as she looked up to Paul and mouthed "thank you" over and over.

Love has many forms, but Lottie and Tom will always recall the sheer intensity of the adoration shining from Joan's eyes into the weary yet exuberant face of Paul, soon to be her husband and already a doting father to their four children. In danger of bringing on another fit of hysterics, we gently led the new family up the stairs to Lottie's now overflowing but jubilant room.

20.   Patience

...imitate those who through faith and patience inherit what has been promised. Hebrews 6:11-13

The group waited for what seemed days in the crowded room where the sounds of the tragedy were muffled but still awful to hear. It really was only one night. Nerves were raw despite the surface cordiality. The youngsters were bored and restless in this unexpected confinement, no matter how many games and books Mary Ellen found for them from back cabinets. The elderly inmates, too, were fidgety to be back to their familiar haunts despite knowing they did little other than sit and wait much as they were doing now only in their own homes. That daily lethargy at least rang with the comfort of familiarity. The change in routine was daunting and drained them. Everyone strained to maintain hope for a swift return to normalcy they had little evidence would prove true in the end of this ordeal.

After their celebratory *meal* of crackers and cheese when Joan, Paul, and the children arrived, the spontaneous refuges ate sparingly of the food stores Robert and Mary Ellen had brought to the room. None of the adults would admit to hunger, and the children seemed as little interested in the mix of odd choices as the cautious adults. They ended up eating pickles and dried apples because those were most plentiful.

In actuality, the dawn would appear a few hours after the rescuers brought in Mrs. Coverdale's two missing children, Laura, her youngest daughter, and Brian, her oldest son. As they waited for daybreak, Paul told the harrowing story of their escape from waters that seemed to come from nowhere with a force none of the others could imagine even with the proof sitting in front of them.

"We were all together at first in the bakery taking things out of the window cabinet just in case we had a leak. I figured being on the second floor would keep us from anything really damaging the water could do. We weren't all that serious about it, I guess," Paul said as he uttered a cough-like laugh, and Joan attempted a weak smile shaking her head slightly.

"I was storing some baking pans," Joan added as they recalled the beginning of this nightmare adventure. The younger children crept closer to their mother. The others were a rapt audience, as if this were some fantastical tale created by a master storyteller. Joan seemed attentive to the talk and questions, but she simultaneously kept up a gentle round of touching all her brood every few seconds, casting off her treasures in the reassurance of her maternal caress. It resembled a mother bird meticulously preening feathers. Looking up, Joan spoke to Paul, "I must have dropped something. Is that when you felt the floor shaking?"

"No. I remember you doing that. It was something made of china or glass, wasn't it?" Paul answered so deep in their memory the others seemed curious interlopers somehow. "When that plate fell and broke, I saw Katie leaning to keep her balance, and my mind just wouldn't put it all together. I thought she was being silly, and I started to tease her. Do you remember that Katie-bug?"

Paul smiled at the girl's timid nod, not sure even yet if she'd somehow done something to bring about the chaos coming so sharply back into focus in their minds right now.

Brian broke the quiet this time. "Dr. Paul," he asked from his perch by his mother's feet, "how *did* the water get up to us when it broke the window? It wasn't flooded that high when we went downstairs later."

"I don't know, Son," Paul answered.

Robert smiled at the young boy who had earned the love and respect of us all with his bravery; he said, "I imagine it must have been the wind, Master Brian. The squalls can carry a wave of water much farther inland than where the Upper Crust sits. And this wind is the strongest I've ever seen here."

"The building itself was shaking?" Mary Ellen asked no one in particular, eager to hear more of how this new extension of her many charges had come to her.

Joan nodded, reaching for another head to touch as she resumed the story, "It was incredible. The floors and walls started moving like...like—I don't know how to even say what it was like. I can still feel it, but...."

"Like when the train first starts and the boards shake under your feet," Michael offered as the others searched their minds for comparable events for so many strange sensations the storytellers were trying to convey.

"It *was* like that, Mike," Paul agreed. "And then the next instant, it felt like the rumble in the floor was a ship going over rough waves, but it wasn't that either."

"I just remember," Joan picked up again, "when we both realized we needed to get everyone down the stairs before that choice was made for us!"

"Exactly," Paul spoke slightly faster, a little less in control as waves of memory crashed down on all of them. "I know the image of St. Pat's flashed into my mind as a solid shelter for us, and I was trying to figure out the best route when the window's plate glass shattered, and we were all sprayed with water."

Laura whimpered softly, and Joan pulled her onto her lap, combing down the already smooth blonde hair.

"I've never heard anything so loud. Have you, Laura?" Joan asked as she continued stroking. She looked at Paul and said, "But I did hear you say 'St. Pat's' before we started down the stairs."

"Me, too," Katie and Michael chimed in to reconstruct their part of the memory.

Brian nodded looking at Lottie, "That's when Dr. Paul told us to get downstairs and try to hold onto each other. I grabbed Laura because she was closest, but I thought we were all together on the stairs. I wasn't trying to get away from anybody. I just kind of slipped, I guess. I don't know what happened really."

"Me, too, Sweetheart," Joan told Brian. "You didn't do anything wrong. That wind was so strong, and then the rain kept coming down. Thank God you picked up little Laura!" The others nodded sympathetically, thinking of how her waifish shape could have slipped so easily away to be lost forever.

Laura finally joined as all of them spewed out the harrowing details. She said, "I couldn't even see anyone else on the stairs or the porch because it was so dark and the rain kept getting in my eyes. I held onto

Brian's green shirt as hard as I could. It hurt my fingers, but I didn't let go."

Paul nodded, hearing the children's amazing stories for the first time along with the others. He managed a choked whisper, "You did a great job, too, Laura—just exactly what you should have done. I'm very proud of you."

"I thought we were all just going to walk over to St. Patrick's," Katie continued the thread, "and that Dr. Paul could put me down once we got down the stairs."

"I could have walked," Michael added.

Joan tousled Michael's now dry hair and teased, "Well, I couldn't! Maybe we should have switched places, and you could carry me!"

Michael smiled at his mother's nonsense and settled more comfortably basking in her attention and nearness.

"But when I got to the porch, I stepped off the last step, I think," Brian kept the narrative going, "But I went down into water."

"How deep was it, Brian?" Tom asked.

Brian looked up at the question and broke momentarily out of his reverie, "I...uh...I guess...it was about up to my knees, I guess. But I jumped back up to the porch real fast and got into Dr. Paul's office to wait for the others."

"The door wasn't even closed," Laura spoke quietly still as if very concerned with this apparent lapse in security. "Didn't you close your door before you came up to the bakery, Dr. Paul? Your pretty chair was all wet."

Paul smiled at her innocent absurdity, "Well, I did, Sweetie, but I think the wind that broke our window in the bakery opened my door, too. I'm starting to think we were mighty lucky the wind didn't blow us all over the place."

"I wonder what the bakery will look like when this is all over," Joan mused.

"I bet it will be a big mess, Mama," Laura chimed in, warming to her role in the adventure now that the feel of her mother's arms assured her she would be safe again.

"We just started picking up all the silver tools Dr. Paul always keeps lined up in that case by the door," Brian retold. "They were all scattered on the floor, and I kept thinking how sorry you would be if somebody walked on them, so we grabbed as many as we could."

Little Laura looked finally peaceful and calm as she slept where she had been sitting curled against

Joan's embrace. The adults had all lowered their voices as the children found a modicum of repose dozing. Tom wondered what teeming images must be forming and reforming in their child eyes—attempts at making sense of the chaos they had just experienced. And Tom had just leaned in to share these thoughts with Lottie when the whole group was startled by the clear, loud voice Laura used when she sat bolt upright exclaiming, "The cows were so funny though, weren't they?"

Her glazed eyes and rigid torso belied her strong voice, and a casual observer would be excused for thinking her fully cognizant of her actions.

Paul spoke softly to the child, "What cows, Laura?"

"You remember, Brian!" Laura smiled in her eerie half-awake state, obviously worlds away from us. As soon as the words were out, she fell back into her fitful slumber again, snoring slightly.

The adults glanced at Brian who nodded but seemed worried about his sister. "Is she OK, Mom? She's acting odd," he asked.

Joan smiled as she readjusted her arm around Laura's shoulder, "She's fine, Sweetheart. She's almost dreaming out loud, but something has a tight hold on her mind, doesn't it?"

Michael stared at Laura, half afraid, half impressed, "You mean she's still asleep but she's talking? How can she do that? Have I ever done that? Is she *really* asleep?"

Paul laughed softly, "Well, in a way, yes. Most people just stay totally asleep when they dream, but she's had quite a day, so her dreams are trying to figure it all out. What does she mean about funny cows, Brian? Do you know what she's talking about?"

Brian nodded, but tears formed in the corners of his eyes and he looked almost sick. His voice was hoarse as he whispered, "It wasn't funny." He choked on the last sound before looking at Paul and then at Joan.

Suddenly, he hurried through his version of the images he and his sister shared. He blurted, "The cow we saw was swimming at first and trying to keep up with us, but he didn't like the water being so high, I think. He kept trying to jump out of the water, but...."

Joan looked over Laura's head at Paul, shaking her head slightly in a mixed response of concern and fear.

Paul's eyes registered the gist and spoke to Brian, emitting all of the love of a parent to his own child, "You don't have to tell us, Brian, if you don't want to."

Brian tried to smile, but he had a look on his face that struggled between revulsion and anger. "I told Laura the cow was just swimming because she was getting so scared at the cow's screaming. It wasn't a moo like a regular cow makes. I didn't know a cow made this kind of noise." Brian couldn't stop now that he'd started talking.

"Then all of a sudden, the cow stopped screaming." Brian continued. "But that wasn't better like I thought it would be at all. Laura wanted to help the cow because she said it must be hurt and that's why it was crying. She kept squirming." Brian took a shuddering breath and finally allowed his tears to fall.

Paul took the still-sleeping Laura in his arms as Joan moved to embrace Brian in a move the couple intuitively choreographed through a love and understanding of how best to hold firm the fragile hearts under their care.

"Shhh," Joan crooned to her first born as if he were still an infant in arms rather than the near-man who certainly had aged considerably in this last day.

She drew his face away from her wet shoulder gently but firmly to look into his eyes. She said, "You, my brave hero son, saved your baby sister's life. I will always owe you a tremendous debt of gratitude. I hate to think what we would be doing now if we had lost any of you instead of just waiting out the storm here all together and dry and comfortable." Ignoring her tears, she took the others in as she told Brian, "The rest of us truly can never know what happened to you while we were apart. What's bothering you about this cow, Darling? Is it just too sad to remember?"

Brian took another breath, emboldened by his mother's faith, "I think…oh, Mama, the cow died, didn't it? It stopped screaming and jumping around and then pretty soon its legs were floating up in the air. The water wasn't too rough at that part. I couldn't see any people or houses or anything. Where were we? And the cow's legs were just there—the way they shouldn't be really. Laura started crying and shaking. I was so afraid I would drop her off that little raft we were floating on. So I told her the cow was just being silly. I didn't know it was dead though, but it was, wasn't it? I'm sorry, Mama; I'm sorry."

Through Joan's murmured shushing, tears coming down her cheeks now, Brian breathed a huge sigh and continued, "When I said that about the silly cow Laura laughed and quit squirming. But it wasn't funny. I don't want to see it anymore, Mama."

"I know, I know," Joan rocked Brian in her embrace, realizing no words could penetrate this grief and horror. Perhaps love and compassion can truly only formulate in the unexpected aftershock of tragedy. Joan never stopped to analyze whether the glow of her love would be worth the agony. She couldn't know if this child who taught her how to love without reserve would be able to stifle the screams of the dying animal obviously etched in his tender ears with the feather touch of this mother's murmurs holding him now in a suspended web of safety and immaterial warmth. She only knew this was her place. The others were insignificant and monotonous intruders in this fleeting moment of perfection.

Compassion formed around Paul's words: "That was brilliant, Brian. You must have worked so hard and so fast to have come up with that clever idea to distract Laura for her own safety." The rest of the group nodded together, feeling inadequate glimpsing the effects this night would have on so many lives. Paul went on, expressing a pride he could ill-disguise, "Didn't you hear her deep memory of it? It's a happy, gentle picture in her mind. She couldn't have made up that good feeling in her dreams. You took away the terror for her Brian and took it on yourself. What an incredibly brave man you are. I am so proud of you."

Joan smiled as Brian blushed at hearing such overt praise.

How the miracle transpired to bring this scattered group together again didn't concern the clannish group, they simply cried and prayed together praising God's mercy. They knew from this momentary glance at the storm and its power that many other families would not be so fortunate. How could miracles with this much intervention be happening all over the island against such an unexpected and fierce enemy? They had no idea the extent of the loss as they held each other and waited for the storm to pass.

"This storm is going to have more of an impact than I could have even expected had we been warned anything was coming into the Gulf," Tom said to Lottie, Paul, and Warren around 3 AM. The others were attempting to sleep all around so they spoke in weary whispers.

"If what we experienced is any indication," Paul responded, "the whole island will be devastated. The stairway going from my office up to Joan's bakery collapsed more from the force of the wind I'm sure. The water was beginning to flood, but we could have waded out but for the wind—that's why we decided to stay in place. Joan has sat out overflows before this with minimal damage. Who would have thought the waves would come up so fast?"

Lottie patted Paul's arm, "You did all the right things, Paul. And God rewarded you for your faith by reuniting all of you. I will never forget this show of God's incredible mercy. What a miracle. Joan was telling me earlier how kind you've been to her and to her children. There's a special place in heaven for men who take care of widows and children; I'm sure of it."

"Before tonight," Paul smiled at Joan, "I assumed we would eventually arrange to come together as a family at some point in the future. Now I know in my heart, we'll never be separated. I wonder how long it will take for Father Liam to have the church back in order to perform the ceremony."

"Get in line, Buddy," Tom teased, winking at a beautifully blushing Lottie. "Just before you sent up your rather boisterous calling card earlier tonight, my darling Miss Gallagher here agreed to make me the happiest of men. I daresay, this evening's events will speed up our timeline as well."

"Ah," Paul exclaimed, smiling again. "Congratulations! I am truly happy for you. We'll certainly all have stories to tell our children, won't we?"

Lottie suddenly became serious again in the next revolution of the emotional wheel each of them had been riding all day. "I do wish we could get out and make sure the sisters and the children are safe at St. Mary's."

"Surely the new dormitories will be fine," Joan Coverdale said softly as she moved next to Paul from where she had settled the children.

Without hesitation or reserve, Paul took her hand and said, "If this were a typical storm, I'd agree, but this is wild. All we can do is pray."

"When can we go out, Tom?" Lottie smiled at Joan as she joined our small group.

"I'm not sure," Tom answered. "Robert will have a better sense of it. I think the wind is dying down from what I can hear inside this room. We certainly can do nothing until we have daylight to guide us. We should all try to sleep. God only knows what we're going to find."

21. Dawn

Then the righteous will shine like the sun in the kingdom of their Father. Matthew 13:43

Waking to the sunlight peeking through the chinks of the window covering, Tom lay still and smiled to see Lottie close to him with her delicate hand lingering on his sleeve. How lovely she looked. She must have sensed Tom's stare and reluctantly opened her sleep-starved eyes, but rewarded him with a comfortable smile.

They both ached as they rose from the mat of blankets that had served as a makeshift bed for their hours-long nap on the floor of Lottie's commodious bedroom. When the time came to sleep, no one wanted to leave the others and rest in any of the other rooms that likely would have been safe enough and certainly more restful. Almost simultaneously, they all chose to forego the comfort of real beds in other parts of the house for the security of proximity to the close-knit group. Lottie had insisted, and the others concurred, that her large bed with the down spreads be reserved for Mrs. Hoglen and Mrs. Kelsey, who claimed they would never be able to sleep but snored methodically soon after their assurances. The others had paired off, making do with odd blankets, quilts, and mismatched bed linens to create nests. Paul and Joan's covey fell together haphazardly near the empty fireplace as if a litter of tired pups congregating on the warm hearth, happy to be whole, lolling into each other in the security of touch.

Lottie nudged Tom's shoulder as he apprised the now-quiet arrangements. She directed her smiling face toward the stalwart Robert sleeping peacefully, who uncharacteristically held a content Mary Ellen in his protective arms. Social regulations and restrictions were relaxed and brought on such a beautiful intimacy, and they knew this would be their silver lining as they recovered from this tragedy. Mrs. Laraby slept on the sofa cradling each of her boys in the crook of her arms. Sheryl held Sophie, and Warren leaned beside her chair nestling Charlie across his chest. Sarah and Bridget formed a human bolster totally surrounding Baby Susanne on her palette murmuring in her sleep. At least for these collected children, all was soft and safe.

Smiling contentedly at this peaceful scene and wishing it could linger, Tom was still eager to look out and see how they would move forward. Lottie and Tom made no noise as they crossed the room, but their connection to the others was stronger than the silence.

As if called to action by a rousing bugle, Warren, Robert, and Paul awoke as Tom stood in his place near the door. Trying to disentangle themselves without waking those who held them protectively was only partially successful. The children mumbled, but easily fell back to sleep with a reassuring pat; the women all awoke. Their memories of the night's adventures were not so quickly dulled by weariness.

Leaving the few who were blessedly able to sleep, the group quietly left the room to explore. The rain had obviously stopped for now; they could hear the silence. And despite their best efforts to close off the outside from reaching them and thus exclude all light from coming in, the triumphant brightness pierced the darkness with slivers of hope. They were being heartily invited outside by the same forces that had imprisoned them mere hours before. The couples were cautious at best, but emboldened with this bright tenacity, Tom walked to the front door and began drawing back the massive bolts and removing the protective inner doors.

Whatever they had to face, they would encounter head on with a fortitude the new friends all held up without questioning its origin too stringently. Just as they had acted on impulse in preparing for this storm, riding out its worst, and rescuing their new friends, they would follow their instincts in recovering from it.

They had been inside their own secluded haven for so long, it began to feel as though they truly were the only world that existed. Could it have only been one night? Beyond the physical devastation and change to the island, the magnitude of which they were just beginning to grasp, the storm's impact on each of them individually was dawning with the sun.

The others wore a similar expression so Tom could only guess they, too, felt as he did in those first moments. He understood himself more fully than ever before; he realized very few things mattered, and that none of them were things. Where once stood a confused, reserved, voiceless boy who quaked in the face of his destiny, now Tom stood, a man calmly assured of the power to create my own future, rejecting any elements he did not want or need.

Robert, Paul, Warren, and Tom, as if symbolic of their new solidarity, pulled together at the large, double doors to stare incredulously at the most affable, gentle, calm dawning any of them could remember witnessing. The day was approaching with no atmospheric sign of the fearful tempest of yesterday. If Friday had been a demonstration of Hell with all her fury, Saturday dawned as Heaven itself, glorious and resplendent. The sun was gracefully rising into a brilliantly bluing sky as they all moved silently onto the porch. Dainty clouds were whisping across the early morning sky playfully, but no threat lingered in their midst, no remnants of the destruction they brought could be seen. The slightest breeze wafted into the close air of the foyer hinting of dampness, and the quiet was not quite natural. No gulls called to each other in the morning air as on a typical Galveston dawn.

For several seconds, none of the small group said anything either. They all stood just outside the wide opening of Cashlin staring upward at the calm sky, waiting for some unknown sign. Then Joan smiled and as if in prayer, said, "God is so good; it truly is over."

Everyone then seemed to talk at once in their joy and relief. They laughed and hugged, shook hands, and slapped backs. They would be a family from this day forward and would tell their separate extended families many stories about that fateful night and the days and weeks and months to come. Some of the stories were sad, but mostly they recalled how together and whole they felt at that moment on the porch, standing once again in the calm sunshine.

Robert, as he so often does, voiced the concern they had not yet spoken. He said somberly, "I wonder what we'll find."

What they did find was incredible.

22.   New Day

You see that his faith and his actions were working together, and his faith was made complete by what he did. James 2:22

Immediately, they all wanted to go out and see what the storm had done to their friends and to Galveston. They were animated and antsy, curious and frightened. Looking beyond the minor storm debris littering Cashlin's once pristine lawns, they could see tree limbs down and branches stopped at awkward angles from their destructive path. The tall stone walls around the estate seemed to have kept out the larger debris.

Their beginning was drawing to a poignant close—not an ending certainly, but also not the cloistered liberty they'd known as the tragedy wreaked havoc all around their bliss. Eden was buffeted on all sides with a satanic intensity only God could control. They were only just beginning to understand the reality of this drama when they all faced each other on the porch. Gently touching them all in turn, Lottie drew their attention and pulled their scattered thoughts back to the moment. "Please," she began quietly, "promise me before we all separate into God only knows what beyond our little fortress here that all of you will return later today and consider Cashlin your home while we see how things stand with your own houses. We have plenty of room and our larder is full."

Overnight, on this most momentous of nights, Lottie had turned from a young, impetuous girl without much direction to a sure-footed woman who began this day to combine her already generous nature with an unlimited capacity to serve others.

Sheryl broke from her husband's side and took Lottie in her trembling arms. "Dear, dear Lottie. You have saved my family, and I will always know that in my heart; you truly are my sister. We'll come back tonight. I know Warren needs to see about the paper and get back to work. Our little cottage will be a mess for sure so close to the shore. But we'll come back tonight."

Lottie beamed at her friend, "Well, leave the babies. We'll be figuring out what all we need to do about provisions, and Mary Ellen will help me. You'll be able to make better time and assess any damage more efficiently without them, and we have plenty of games and toys in the attic. I want to get over to St. Mary's as soon as the men can get out and see how the sisters fared. We'll likely have a house full of children and nuns when you return!"

Tom stood in awe, watching her. Even in this most turbulent and emotional of moments, her thoughts were on practicalities and on easing the burdens of others. His admiring stare caught her attention, and Tom was rewarded with a loving smile and a slight blush.

"Tom," she began to the others, "would you lead us in a prayer? I think we're all going to need a lot of reminding for the next couple of days that we need to call on God to help us."

"That's good," Warren proclaimed on the echo of their Amen. "That will help all of us."

There was nothing to do but start, so they left in twos and threes to find what this unforgettable storm had done to their beloved island. The area immediately around Cashlin seemed bruised but not extensively damaged. Tom was beginning to think perhaps the fury they heard had been more melodramatic than substantial, but some gut feeling assured him they had not survived mere histrionics.

Sheryl and Warren left the children sleeping upstairs. And Lottie began to organize Mary Ellen and Sarah. Mrs. Laraby was intent on leaving to find her husband, so Robert took her clan to their own home.

Tom walked with Paul toward St. Patrick's to ascertain Liam's safety. Each block confirmed their worsening fears. Paul spoke first, "I don't know what I thought we'd see. I know from the muffled noises last night and just what Joan and I saw before we got to you that we would see something like this, but I hadn't expected it to be everywhere."

Tom nodded as they walked near the root end of a stories-high tree lolling across what the day before had been a busy commercial thoroughfare. The way was littered with mostly unidentifiable debris. The men would later reason that they couldn't tell what it was initially because most of what was on the lawns and dangling from the trees and atop fences should never have been outside. It was the shredded remains of quilts lovingly stitched by nameless grandmothers from somewhere in Nebraska. There was the top of a writing desk splintered into unnatural shapes. Tin soldiers detached forever from their nursery regiments. Cooking utensils. Wisps of lace. Letters. Shards of glass. Pictures. A solitary porcelain tea cup eerily intact. In only a few blocks, their dulled senses had encountered several downed trees, and they no longer stopped to stare and try to identify their own location. Akin, Tom imagined, to armies in the aftermath of fierce battle, they moved forward automatically in mute shock at what their vision declared true but their minds could scarce process or in any way comprehend.

They saw a few other tentative searchers moving in a daze. Despite the innate comfort of seeing their fellow survivors, no one spoke; silently acknowledging each other, they could find no words for what they saw. Shocked faces told silent stories more grim than what even Paul had lived.

Debris was everywhere. Familiar streets seemed not to run parallel to others they had used only days before. Landmark buildings were no longer standing where Tom knew they should be. Many lots were filled with debris, but some areas were totally clear. No structure, no family, no history.

Homes stood embarrassed by their nakedness, missing porches and chimneys. They could only guess where doors and windows may once have been as absurd openings glared from the battered frames of the houses that were still standing. Siding had been stripped so they could see into a cozy room with skewed furniture succumbing to the wild wind that had lashed the home. Then they would be baffled to see lace curtains whisping in and out of gaping holes coyly showing an undisturbed dish cabinet defiantly standing sentry over its fragile porcelain. Had it not been so incredibly depressing to delve too deeply into what had caused this mayhem, the mental exercise of determining what had actually happened from one edifice to another and from one block to another may have been exhilarating, but the reality of the losses was too fresh. Their fascination was tempered, and Paul and Tom knew they would soon hear stories of the human suffering beyond any imagined scenarios that resulted in these fascinating piles and formations.

They could see very little of the roads. Lawn and road merged under the scattered remains of orderly lives torn asunder. One pile of tree branches and eerie shapes gave way to another mound grotesquely mimicking nature but unreal in its haphazard composition. One such collection impeded their progress by its sheer enormity. Nothing seemed normal, and the realization of the all-inclusive destruction came over the men in waves of nausea. Staring at a screen door forced into the top edge of the pile, they both heard the whimper.

"What is that?" Tom asked Paul, choking down an outburst of hysteria that had threatened to surface at each turn in the road. Aloud, Tom prayed, "Please, God, let that not be a child."

Paul looked at Tom, mirroring his horror. "No," he whispered, "I don't think so. It's an animal of some sort, but where is it coming from?" Another whisper of sound.

"Over here," Tom screamed, glad to put his anxiety into action. As Tom moved to the tallest side of the chaotic pile, the animal grew louder as if sensing other living creatures nearby. Paul joined in as Tom gingerly lifted pieces off the location he felt more than knew covered the sound they sought. As they progressed, their deconstruction became more aggressive, spending their shock in this fight for life. The pieces they removed formed yet another pile of incongruent combinations—cloth and glass and wood, all soaked and heavy with silt. Peeling away each layer gave a fleeting purpose to their unspoken sense of helplessness and guilt from last night. Unable to move and act beyond their privileged enclave as the storm controlled their movements, they had suffered but could provide little aid to anyone else, but now they could exert again.

Tom was jubilant when Paul pulled away the final branch that had trapped the young, brown pup. Paul scooped up the dog triumphantly as they both laughed at their small victory. The rescued animal immediately responded by jumping down and pawing Paul's leg, licking his hand, and yelping his thanks.

"He seems no worse for wear," Tom smiled. "Looks like the kids will have a new buddy."

Paul smiled and looked up from scratching the dog's ears. He said, "I daresay we'd be hard pressed to get away from here without him, that's for sure. I wonder if we should look for his owner."

The thought sobered them immediately; the devastation they were only beginning to see would have extracted a heavy toll on their neighbors with less substantial homes than the stone fortress Daniel had built Cashlin to be.

"I think it will be all right if he wants to follow us," Tom said quietly, ignoring the sorrow he was beginning to piece together. "What do you think the kids will want to name him?"

They were moving toward St. Pat's again with their rescued friend close on their heels, as predicted. He scampered and explored, but never strayed far from Paul.

Paul picked up on Tom's desire to stay focused on the future and beyond or risk being mired in the emotional enormity of what they had experienced. He began, "Well, when the storm started coming and we thought we would have a good long time to just sit, Joan started reading the kids *The Tempest* again. They read it aloud a lot, I guess. So I suppose the girls will want 'Miranda' but Michael will put in for 'Ariel'—

that's his favorite character, and he gets to play him when they read the parts out."

"That's pretty highfalutin,'" Tom smiled. "I was thinking something like 'Lucky' or 'Stormy,' but I guess that's pretty unoriginal!"

As they walked on what they remembered to have been the last street before St. Patrick's, they both slowed down. With no exchange of words, they stopped, and seemed to understand some inner need to pause for breath before they moved forward to discover the next obstacle.

Paul turned and said, "Tom, I know you're better at this than I am, but would you mind if I said a prayer before we go see about Father Liam and the others at the church?"

"I know that would help me," Tom answered. They prayed together and started to move on. Tom realized he had never prayed so much and so fervently outside a church in his life.

Later when Tom was telling Lottie about their trip to St. Pat's, he remembered saying how glad he was to be distracted, first by Paul's request and again just before they turned the corner to face the imposing church. Watching the antics of the liberated and fortunate dog, Paul and Tom momentarily forgot the devastation. Every image they saw jarred them into a deeper recognition of the chaos they were finding everywhere.

Suddenly, Tom heard his name but couldn't see anyone until he turned around to see William DeHaven running quickly towards them, relief obvious in the teen's smiling face.

"Mr. Tom," he panted, still running. "Mr. Tom—we found you!" William and a smaller boy Tom knew by sight to be from St. Mary's but could never place stopped before the men totally disheveled. Wet hair, wild clothing, and scraped arms and legs, the boys stood barefooted and out of breath.

"Wills," Tom clapped his back in a tight embrace, shocked relief mingled with affection and pride. "You're safe. Thank God!" Come with us to St. Pat's, then we'll take you home with us—Miss Lottie will be so happy to see you. She fretted after all of you last night."

"Yes, Mr. Tom, but..." William stammered and suddenly burst into sobs long withheld.

Not even attempting to stem the tears, Tom looked at Paul over the boy's shoulder, knowing they both were sharing his tearful release in their own ways. As Tom held the young man in his arms, he was tempted to send him immediately on to Lottie; Tom knew she would better be able to soothe him, but Tom felt keenly Wills would want to stay with the men now that he had found familiar faces out of the wreckage. Deciding on the instant, Paul and Tom kept the boys with them, wanting to hear their story, but also needing to ascertain that Liam was well. Wills couldn't talk of his ordeal yet anyway; he just kept mumbling. Tom caught only "gone" and "tried" but didn't press him. More than at any point on their exhausting walk, Tom longed to be with Lottie again. She would know how to make sense of all these unconnected bits. They hurried along.

No matter how artfully they could have stalled, no matter how many distractions they could have encountered, and no matter how long they could have put off rounding the last corner in their fear of seeing some unknown damage to their beloved church, nothing would have prepared them for the awful image of the battered ruins of St. Patrick's. Tom groaned as if struck to see the gaping wound where the tall roof once stood proud in its ostentatious display of spirituality. Paul reeled beside his friend and grasped Tom's shoulder to steady them both. The boys were silent—terror streaking their young faces with pictures too gruesome to believe yet hauntingly real. What power could cause such heart-wrenching destruction?

The new bell tower, such a point of pride for the parish, remained complete on the building's end, but closer inspection of one side showed crumbled stone at the top of the Gothic block as if a mighty chisel were fashioning a new design out of the solid form. In the span between the disheveled tower and what had been the altar, only parts of the roof clung to the arched window walls. From where they stood, the group could see no steeple, no stained glass, and no sign of life. All Tom could think of was "Tintern Abbey" and all Wordsworth's wandering ghosts. But Tom didn't want to think of ghosts right then; the image was too real.

All four of them broke the terrifying spell at once calling, "Father Liam" over and over as them ran to the rubble.

"Spread out and be careful," Tom shouted as they reached the still high side walls amidst rubble of cloth and wood and stone much like the debris piles they had encountered along the way earlier. Somehow these ruined treasures were sadder though in their ravished sacredness.

Tom forced away his tears for fear of succumbing to the breakdown he sensed resided just under the surface and recognized that he had been repeating this controlling gesture all morning. He moved on, comforted, knowing he would always have Lottie to help him unravel the confusion.

Paul was first to come upon Liam searching meticulously through the rubble of the church building. After their relieved greetings, Liam told them the first tragedy the storm had presented to us: Father O'Mallary was missing. Through his shock, Tom wondered how many more friends and whole families they would come to find were no longer where they had been before some element of the fierce storm had taken them off. These missing became a haunting memory of what once was real and no longer remained. Tom's animosity at the old man's injustice to him from only yesterday flashed into Tom's mind mocking him with its intensity now that he could see so clearly how any slight toward another was meaningless. Their grasp on this reality is so fragile; Tom knew with certainty then he would never see the old priest again and felt an ache of remorse.

The crazed scene before them offered no answers immediately other than the bright sun warming the day. They were alive, and they were together. They could only hold fast to these solitary blessings and move forward.

23.   Tomorrow

...the new creation has come: The old has gone, the new
is here!" 2 Corinthians 5:17

With promises to return after they reported their findings, Tom's group left Liam organizing the growing number of parishioners coming to the decimated church who would depend on him to lead them back to some sort of normalcy. They hurried back to Cashlin to connect with their own fabricated comfort in the chaos. Lottie had been watching for their return and ran down the wide stairs to meet the men as they opened the front doors. Tom quickly assured her Liam was safe and relinquished William to her eager grasp.

"William! Oh, thank you, God!" Lottie held Wills in a maternal hug that did more for his emotional recovery than any medicine could have. The silent angst was released. He welcomed the chance to tell Lottie all he had seen.

"I tried so hard, Miss Lottie," he struggled to clear his voice of the tears hovering on each syllable as the words gushed forward, "really, I did. But I just couldn't. The water came so fast. I've never seen it like that before. I figured we were so high up, and Mother Superior didn't want the little ones to be scared. But they were anyway, and even some of the sisters were crying."

Lottie, so much more adept at allowing time for the pauses people need to recall their thoughts, didn't interrupt or try to prompt him; she just waited with a sad look of resignation on her face. Her one darling was here, but what of all the others?

"When we moved all the children up to the third floor, I knew we'd be safe," Wills continued. "Then Mother had all the sisters take a few children together, and they...they tied the rope I had gotten out of the shed around them and then onto the little kids so they could stay together."

"I think Mother knew the water was getting higher," Wills was almost whispering as the others listened in silent dread. If for any end to this tale other than the most dire, he would have told us where the others were by now, surely, Tom realized. So Tom sat with the others waiting to hear what he couldn't stand to imagine.

Lottie understood how important it was for Wills to tell us and not keep the images inside. She had let him tell the details, but realized now he needed help. "The sisters sometimes did that for long walks, didn't they, William? They called it a daisy chain so the wee ones would hold on. To keep everyone together."

"Yes, ma'am, Miss Lottie," he said, but wouldn't look at her. "It was just like a walk, and the children were excited, I think, because just staying up there was starting to become even more scary than the sounds outside." Again, Wills stopped and seemed at a loss for words.

Tom asked quietly, "But you and Albert didn't get in with the others?" Tom looked at the young boy who had been with Wills when they had found the men earlier and smiled.

Wills looked up with gratitude, "That's it. We didn't. We're bigger, so Mother said we didn't need as much help as the little ones. Me and Albert and Frank, we didn't. But there seemed to be so many others. The sisters made slings around their necks out of their work aprons to carry to babies, and held the hands of the others and they were all tied together. Sometimes they kept singing and sometimes saying prayers over and over. It was a mess, but then I was so glad they were all connected because all of a sudden, like a big crash, the water started coming in one window and the wall just started breaking. We were so high. How did the water get up so high, Miss Lottie?" he brushed away the tears that would come despite his efforts.

Lottie was crying now, too, and said, "I don't know, Sweet Angel; I don't know." She was still holding Wills as they sat together on the bench in the entryway of Cashlin. The ornate entry doors stood open with a gentle summer breeze wafting through in mocking contrast to the storm just hours before that had caused such tragedy. Sounds they could only imagine echoed in their minds: breaking glass, cracking wood, rushing water. Familiar, similar, yet so drastically alien. All at once and so violent. The gentle light beams in the opulent foyer played off the shining surfaces as if to temper the sobriety of its occupants. "What happened when the water came in, Sweetheart?"

"It were awful loud," Albert spoke the first words they had heard him utter all morning.

Wills picked up again, "Yeah. Real loud. The wall just started...it started...I don't know, Miss Lottie, Mr. Tom, it just weren't a wall then. One minute it was up there just like regular, and then it weren't nomore. That's when the screaming started."

The adults all hung on the horrifying images these broken words were forming for them. Wills started again, more steadily now, but also more quickly, "The water came in the room and the sisters gathered all the children they had tied close to them. Mother was praying louder than before, and all the whole long line of them started floating away."

Albert joined in again, unable not to, "At first it looked like fun, like at the beach, huh Wills? Didn't it look like they were just going for a swim?"

Wills nodded but then continued, "But real quick like, I knew it weren't good, Miss Lottie." He started crying in earnest now, and they all suffered with him as the sisters and their young charges swept away from the shelter that had relied on to keep them safe and dry. Joan shuddered as she wept.

"They just kept going like they couldn't get upright," Wills painted the grim picture. "As soon as it started, I tried to stop them and see if we could get some place higher together, but the water was going so fast and then the rain started coming harder and the wind wouldn't stop. There weren't no time to think and make a plan. I couldn't hear nothing, it were so loud. Me and Frank and Albert ended up holding on in a tree right by the window but the little ones were gone by then. And the sisters. All of them."

Joan spoke quietly but with the faith her recent miracle had emboldened. "We'll find them, William. The men will go look again soon."

William tried to smile his thanks, but failed. "The babies they can't swim you know. I tried to catch them, Miss Lottie. I promise I tried. They were going under the water a lot and the sisters would grab 'em up again, but it was all so fast."

Lottie looked at Tom over Wills's shoulder. Her voice caught on his name, but she steadied herself, "William, Darling. Look at me now, Sweetheart. You did everything you could to help the others. You and Albert were very brave, and I am so proud of you. Mr. Tom and Dr. Paul will keep looking for all the children; I'm sure the sisters were able to get them to a safe place all together. You're both going to stay here now and help me. Do you understand?"

Both boys nodded and tried to stem their memory-filled tears. Lottie once again guided them all so they wouldn't stay rooted in the tragic pictures uppermost in their minds. "Mr. Tom will help you boys find some clothes in my brother's room, then Miss Mary Ellen will get you something to eat because we have a lot of work to do. Father Liam will need us to help when people need a place to sleep tonight. Let's get started."

The prospect of meaningful activity roused them all, and they filed the disturbing thoughts Wills's story had conjured away to contemplate later. They knew they could never forget, but they could postpone.

And so they did. They started. They began the slow and painful process of righting their overturned world. They pushed down images they could not endure with the force of how enormous the task was before them. They soothed nightmares they could not ignore.

With few words and no arguments, they made arrangements for sleeping, eating, and living. Old rules and restrictions gave way to the dire necessity for the survivors to push forward.

They grieved for all they had lost, and rejoiced for all they found safe. No one who lived would ever be the same. Galveston would never be the same. Knowing the power that both gave and took away strengthened them all. They moved forward with their separate lives as a family united through fear and suffering to create a bond even death will not sever.

That's how Lottie and Tom came to be. Very soon after the storm, Father Liam married them alongside Paul and Joan in the most joyous, boisterous day of their lives. The hopeful freshness of their unions was contagious as they all walked back to Cashlin from the cathedral. Their fast friends and new neighbors longed to share in their determination to set aside the silt and destruction and focus on true priorities.